HIGHLAND SECRETS
Shaws & Macrobs, Book 3
Published by Keira Montclair
Copyright © 2022 by Keira Montclair

This is a work of fiction. Names, characters, places and incidents are either the product of the author's imagination or are used fictitiously, and any resemblance to actual persons, living or dead, business establishments, events or locales is entirely coincidental.

Printed in the USA.

Cover Design and Interior Format

© KILLION
THE
GROUP, INC.

HIGHLAND SECRETS

SHAWS & MACROBS — BOOK 3

KEIRA MONTCLAIR

TO THE READER:

The Shaws and MacRobs trilogy follows three couples as they find unexpected love in the midst of an ongoing clan conflict. While each couple gets an HEA at the end of their story, the mystery behind the feud carries across all three books. For the best experience, reading the series in order is strongly recommended.

~

Shaws and MacRobs Trilogy:
Highland Feud (Book 1) by Emma Prince
Highland Seduction (Book 2) by Cecelia Mecca
Highland Secrets (Book 3) by Keira Montclair

CHAPTER ONE

Early June 1245, The Highlands of Scotland

RHONA SHAW MACADDER entered the hunting lodge deep in the forest behind Castle MacRob, the stronghold of the clan that the Shaws hated the most. She'd never belonged among her husband's clan anyway, so she kept as far away from the MacAdders as possible.

The feud between the Shaws and MacRobs continued to grow, fueled first by the disappearance of two people, one a Shaw and the other a MacRob, and fanned even higher by King Alexander himself. Rhona had been there at the beginning, twelve years ago, when her brother, new laird of Clan Shaw, had forced her to marry a man she hated, Duncan MacAdder, instead of the one she loved, Royce MacRob. Up until her brother's edict, she and Royce, both twenty summers old at the time, had carried on for nearly a year with the expectation they would marry soon.

But the death of the Shaw laird, her father, had changed everything.

She rubbed her forehead hard, as if the pressure could stop the pain throbbing there or bring back her missing cousin Ian, though she'd gained nothing from any of the previous thousand times she'd made the gesture.

Ian was missing, and MacRob clan member Marta had disappeared at the same time. Evidence that the two were together had been found near the River Luath. Why were they together? Catlin, her brother's new wife, had uncovered evidence that they were in love and ran away, but the feud was so strong, Rhona wasn't sure she believed that. Some MacRobs thought Ian forced Marta to go somewhere with him. Some Shaws, in turn, believed Marta used some kind of trickery to lure Ian away. Somewhere along the line, someone had been wounded, because blood had been found near the river, patches of a plaid and a Shaw horseshoe found close by.

Then the healer who had attended her brother's forced wedding had said that someone had stabbed a lass and that the two were heading to Berwick together. Rhona's sister and new husband had guessed the pair were going to visit Marta's aunt, so they'd headed to Berwick over a fortnight ago, hoping to catch sight of the couple, hoping to bring them home and end this foolish feud. But the newly wedded couple should have returned by now. She couldn't help but worry that something may have happened to Tor and her dearest sister, Ainsley.

Her maid, Forsy, had heard the gossip about the healer and passed it on to her. Rhona could no longer stand by and do nothing.

Her skin pricked as if someone were watching her. She stopped in her tracks, turning around to see if the lodge door had opened, but it hadn't. She settled, guessing she was still alone. She'd done her best to clean the place a bit, though it did show signs of someone else having used it more recently than the last time she'd been here, twelve years before.

To her, it was theirs. Royce's and hers. No one else belonged here. She wanted to put a lock on the door, though she had no legal right. It was on MacRob land, after all, and she supposed the laird's family—Royce's family—still made hunting expeditions to this corner of their holdings. Making her way around the main room, she traced a finger across the items that brought back memories.

Wonderful memories.

Sprigs of dried lavender hung from the mantel. A basket full of pinecones on a chest. A warm plaid folded over the back of one chair facing the hearth. Two tallow candles sat in holders on the wall. She lit one of them, because the day was a bit gloomy. She moved to the window, opening the shutter a wee bit with a shiver to peer out into the shadows of the forest. Anyone coming this far would probably carry a torch, even though it was the middle of the day.

One tree in the distance caught her gaze, and a small smile crept onto her lips. Oh, how she remembered that tree. How her lover had held her in his strong hands against that tree, lifting her skirts and plunging into her, a night of sheer ecstasy.

She hadn't been loved like that in years.

The kind of pleasure that made you wish to tear your clothes off and toss them into the hearth. Or rip your lover's clothes off with your teeth. The kind that made you tremble with desire, quake with a need that she'd only felt for one man, scream as that man's talented fingers and tongue plunged her into a climax that would make her forget her name, even where she was.

Everything but the man she was with.

It could have been hers. *He* could have been hers, but she'd walked away.

Not willingly. She had been forced to turn her back on the love of her life.

But he hadn't viewed it that way. He'd never forgiven her. Accused her of choosing another over him, even when he knew she'd had no choice. It had been her laird's command, her only brother. She'd loved her brother with all her heart until the day he'd told her he had agreed to the arranged marriage to a neighboring laird. One who was pure evil.

The man had offered for Ainsley, but she couldn't allow the man to touch her younger sister, who had only been twelve at the time. Her brother Broden had agreed to honor the betrothal her father had arranged with the neighboring laird, unbeknownst to anyone, so Rhona had married the man.

Her love for two men had turned to hatred within a sennight. First for her brother, then her beloved when he refused to understand, accusing her of turning on him. He hadn't believed a word she'd told him—or hadn't been able to truly hear her. So blind with hurt and rage, he couldn't understand her position nor see her own grief.

And he probably never would. That thought didn't help keep back the tears misting her vision, and she whisked them away with her hand, refusing to allow him to see any weakness in her.

She couldn't help but wonder how this meeting would go, or if he would even come. The two of them hadn't been alone together since that fateful day when she'd gone home from their rendezvous and discovered her sire had, before his death, signed a written agreement promising one of his daughters to another man.

Her heart had shattered into a thousand pieces that day. She'd begged her brother to call off the betrothal. The man she was to marry was cold and cruel and much older than she was. But Broden hadn't relented, hadn't been willing to consider any other path.

How she wished their dear mother had still been alive, because she'd never have allowed the marriage, but she had passed away six moons before they lost their father.

Her marriage, begun in sorrow, had ended in hatred. She'd never loved her husband, never had any feelings for the man she'd been forced to marry. Everyone knew it. But she could not admit the corresponding truth that had stayed the same, deep in her core, ever since she and Royce had met. She still loved Royce MacRob with all her heart, with every part of her being, with every breath she took.

She always had, even as she hated him for thinking the worst of her.

~

Royce stopped his horse a distance from the old hunting lodge for an unfamiliar reason and handed the reins to his second, Mungo. "I'll no' be long."

Mungo quirked a brow in question, but Royce ignored him.

He needed to focus on what he was about to face, because he needed to gain control of his emotions before he stepped into this situation. Perhaps walking the rest of the way would help, especially since summer was finally here. He loved the budding of the leaves in spring and the bright colors of early summer.

If he didn't clamp down on his roiling heart and mind, nothing would prevent him from falling to his knees in front of the woman and begging her to return to him, begging her to lie in his arms again. He would hear his name on her lips as she went over the edge, her passion the most arousing sight he'd ever witnessed.

Pushing her over the edge of abandon had lodged in his memory as one of only a few great experiences in his lifetime. He had to lock the memory away or risk losing himself to her again. Every glance at Rhona Shaw, every word that came from her lips could bring him back to those moments of ecstasy, of sharing an experience that only a few understood.

Once, he'd loved her so much that when she walked away, she'd ripped his heart out and stomped on it. That kind of love marks someone for life. And its destruction caused a feud that still raged between two clans that used to be allies. Exactly the reason he'd stayed far away from her for the last twelve years.

After she'd betrayed him by breaking their understanding and marrying another.

Everyone told him her brother had forced the marriage, but to him it was no different than having the woman drive a stake into his heart, allowing what was left of their love to dribble out of him. He'd tried to rid himself of every last memory. Every last word they'd spoken to one another. He was fortunate that he'd rarely seen her in the twelve years they'd been apart.

He'd done all he could to go on as if he were a whole man, and he'd been somewhat successful until . . .

Until that morn when she'd sent a messenger asking for his assistance. Asking him to come to their old trysting place.

What the hell did she want? What could possibly be her game? Her goal?

Why, in heaven's name, had he come?

He stopped at the edge of the clearing, only a short distance away from the tree that had given him one of his fondest memories. Lovesick fools back then, they had carved their initials into a nearby tree's bark. That was something Rhona liked to do, having carved it in another tree previously. In that time, they were powerless to stop their need for each other. The desperation they'd felt had driven them to indecency, and taking his lover against a tree, her skirts around her waist, had ignited a finish he would never feel again.

He tried to tell himself it had been the tree, their position, but he knew better.

It had been everything about Rhona, the woman he loved. Her glazed eyes. Her cries. Her laughter. And her scent, the lavender that he inhaled like it would breathe life into him at the worst times. The scent he wore for hours after, mingling with the memory of her warm breath against his ear, of her nails raking across his shoulder that caused a pain so sweet he'd beg for it.

He'd listened to so many young lads over the years, bragging about the lass with the largest breasts, the finest arse. They were too young to understand the true appeal of a woman. It didn't come from their breasts or their curvaceous bottoms or their pretty faces, but from inside. It was the connection, a man's ability to make her tremble, whimper, beg to be touched in her private places, scream his name in the middle of a climax. It was the way a man and a woman learned to play each other's bodies like the finest harp in the world, knowing what a touch would ignite. Sometimes just a look.

Or the way holding her soft hand in his own had made him feel invincible, strong, powerful.

He'd known it and lost it. Had been so utterly

in love with her that he knew he could never love like that again.

He was halfway across the path before he even realized it. He stopped a distance away from the door. He had to calm his breathing, hating how just the thought of the woman, her mahogany hair falling down her back in waves, her grip on his biceps unrelenting until he brought her to climax, the one word on her lips as sweet as any word he ever heard, even now made him race toward her.

But the look in her blue eyes grabbed him most. *Royce. My sweet Royce, how I love you.* He'd memorized that line and thought of it many times when he was in need of sustenance—on the battlefield, tramping through a snowstorm searching for lost sheep, in his own chamber in the dark of night.

He cursed again under his breath, hating the day he'd received word about her betrothal to someone other than him. He and Rhona hadn't been formally betrothed because her sire had been ill, but they both knew they belonged together. She'd blamed her brother, how he'd been forced to sell her soul to another because of an agreement MacAdder had produced, but he'd never believed it to be true. If she'd wanted a way out badly enough, she could have found it. Broden Shaw was a bastard, sure as he was walking to see the man's sister, and now that bastard was Royce's brother by marriage, thanks to the king's decree.

He'd had to stop thinking about Rhona Shaw.

It was the only way he could survive. And now here he was, standing like a fool and thinking of nothing but her.

He rubbed his chin, reminding himself that he was stronger than he gave himself credit for. Rhona was older, probably not as pretty, not the lithe lass he'd tangled with as a young man. She must have changed in so many ways that once he saw her, he would feel entirely different.

He'd always thought that if he could have spent one more hour with her, made love to her one more time, been able to say a final goodbye, that everything would have been different, and he'd have been able to move on. He was about to find out if he was right.

He caught the glow of a candle inside telling him she had arrived ahead of him, was probably inside waiting for him. Patting the flank of her horse as he approached the door, he stopped for a moment, shaking his head. Thoughts of Rhona Shaw had so overwhelmed him that he hadn't even seen her horse until he had come abreast of it.

He silently thanked whoever had brought her to him one last time.

Even if it was only a horse.

He still loved her as much as he ever had, he realized. And that terrified him.

CHAPTER TWO

RHONA HEARD FOOTSTEPS outside and spun around, leaning her back against the chest she'd been tidying. It was him. It had to be Royce. The firm knock at the door was the same as it had always been, and her body overheated in a powerful reaction to thoughts of this man. A man like no other.

Strong, powerful, steadfast Royce. The kind of man you could count on. The kind of man who knew how to love and how to treat a woman.

Doing her best to hide the tremor in her voice, she quickly fanned her flushed face and said, "Enter."

The door opened, and the man who'd monopolized her dreams for well over a decade filled the doorway. As handsome as ever, he still wore his light brown hair long, and she saw the same wee bit of curl at the ends. He stopped in the doorway until his gaze locked on hers. A few fine lines edged those gorgeous green eyes, which were exactly the same except for a hardness she hadn't seen there before—not when he'd been looking at her, at least. She guessed that new edge had been caused by her marriage to MacAdder.

She hadn't expected him to smile, and when he did, her insides turned to jelly.

She would not cry. She would not embarrass herself.

Muscular. Strong. Delectable. The words shot through her mind, but she forced herself to focus.

She had an important reason for this meeting, and she couldn't dwell on their past, no matter how delicious it was. "Royce, you look well. Please come in."

He nodded and moved into the room, coming no closer to her than necessary. He broke his gaze away from her and trained it on the fireplace. She supposed she deserved that after marrying another. But her husband was dead now, killed in a fall from his horse two years ago. How fitting that an adder had crossed his path, frightening the beast and causing it to rear, throwing the man and snapping his neck.

That gave her true freedom at long last—from her marriage and the fear of being forced back into her abuser's home. With her husband dead, she could allow Royce to touch her whenever and wherever he wished, bring her any of the delicious pleasures they'd shared before. A passing caress was as special to her as their intense lovemaking, and Royce had excelled at both.

He'd always known just how and where to touch her, and she trusted him completely even now. She'd never understood how that one quality was more important than any other until she'd lost it.

Would he touch her at all? Or would his hatred

for her prevent it?

She'd never trusted her husband—not from the moment she first cast eyes on him. Her instincts had proven true.

Forcing Duncan MacAdder out of her mind, she returned her focus to this man in front of her. The only love of her life. If only she could repeat their last time together and change the ending.

"What do ye want, Rhona? State yer business quickly. I'm laird of my clan, and if ye have no' noticed, we have problems."

She clenched her skirt in her fists, but whether to stop her trembling or keep herself from striking him, she did not know. "I am fully aware of the issue involving Ian and Marta. I am not ignorant. It is because of them that I asked you here. We must do what we can to end this foolishness King Alexander has thrust upon our clans."

He leaned against the table and crossed his arms. "And just how do ye propose to do such a thing? We cannae make demands on the king. If 'twere so easy, we'd have done so already. But instead Broden and Catlin married, then Tor and Ainsley. We have nae idea where those two are or if they're even still alive, on top of Ian and Marta having gone missing. What can we do at this point?"

"We cannot allow the king to force any more marriages on our clans. We must stop this." She folded her hands in front of her and stared at him, drinking in all that was Royce MacRob before he disappeared—the strong jawline, the green eyes that would turn to desire whenever she touched him, the lips that could turn her into a puddle at his feet. And how was it possible that she could look at the hair on his legs and have butterflies dashing through her body in response? He still leaned against the table, his legs and arms both crossed now, and she couldn't help but lick her lips.

"This feud started with us. We are the only ones who can end it," she said, hoping he would hear her out.

If she could just have one more view of the hair on his chest, she'd be forever grateful.

Her female parts were betraying her, she swore, traitor to her wishes, to her entire being.

"Nay, the feud had slowed until the discovery that Ian and Marta were missing. Then the fingers all pointed at each other. True that 'tis raging as strong as ever now, but 'tis about more than us. I dinnae think 'tis in our power to end it."

"You always were stubborn. You only saw things from one point of view. Think of your brother being forced to marry my sister. Do you think he was pleased?" She asked her question, but her mind continued to return to his lips, the ones she'd felt in places she'd never have imagined, setting her body alight, casting her inhibitions to the wind. How could she ever forget his lips, his tongue?

And his hands. No one had ever touched her like Royce MacRob. She yearned for that touch again. Could she convince him?

If she dropped her clothes to the floor this instant, what would he do?

She sat down, mostly because her knees would surely buckle if her thoughts kept going in that direction with him so close, close enough for her to take in his scent. That aroma that only he carried, of horse and mint from the leaves he chewed, plus a touch of pine, all mixed with the scent that was simply *Royce*. If only she could find a way to lock it in a bottle.

Being this close to him was affecting her in just the way she'd feared it would. She wanted him—under her, over her, between her legs, against her mouth, every way possible. She could feel the sweat beading across her brow, and she swiped at it in the hopes he'd not see it.

Moistness gathered between her legs, and she feared he would sense it somehow. He'd always been so alert to her desires. Every part of her was awaiting any motion from him, any movement that would tell her he wanted her.

But he gave no sign.

He moved away from her and leaned against the end of the hearth, crossing his arms again. The flicker of the firelight made the hair on his legs stand out one more time. Did the man know how he was torturing her? She recalled a time when she had kissed a line up his calf to his knee, to his thigh, and above. He'd bucked when she'd kissed him *there*, and she'd discovered a power she never knew she had. And that she loved the taste of him.

She licked her lips absentmindedly. As soon as she realized what she'd done, saw his gaze lock on her lips, she turned her head away.

She had to stop staring at him.

Showing him her back, she cleared her throat and spoke her idea, the reason she'd asked him here. "If we married, the feud would be over. Marry me, Royce. We can start anew. My husband is dead. We can pretend the past never happened."

Out of the corner of her eye, she caught him pushing himself away from the hearth and beginning to pace, something he did often when he couldn't make up his mind about something.

"Ye have surely turned daft if ye think I would ever consider such a step." His pace back and forth across the room didn't slow, though, which meant he was considering her proposal. Good. "Or that yer brother would accept our betrothal any more readily now than he did back then."

She had to convince him, and she'd do almost anything to gain his agreement, even allowing him to decide exactly how the marriage would be. "I know the idea might be shocking, but someone must force the king to stop his mad interference. We could ask for an annulment shortly after. We could sleep in separate chambers, stay apart. I'll give you whatever you want if you help me put a stop to this."

"Whate'er I want? Do ye know what ye're offering, lass? Have ye asked yer brother if he would allow it?"

"Nay, I'll not ask him. I'm a grown woman and a widow, and I can do as I wish. He'll see I was right once the feud is ended."

He stopped his pacing to lock gazes with her.

Too close. He was too close, and he knew it

as well as she did, his eyes glazing over with the desire she'd seen so many times before.

It was as if a lightning bolt jumped from her to him and back again, a flare that could not be controlled.

Royce took three steps forward until he stood a bare hand's length in front of her. His scent washed over her, and she had the immediate daft desire to nibble on his shoulder, his neck, feel the muscles in his arms flex beneath her fingers. The way he'd done countless times before. She so wished to see if he still had that wee mole near his right nipple, her eyes traveling there on their own. She gasped when she realized she'd divulged her secret desires to him with just a glance.

She could not control her reaction. Her breathing sped up, the blood in her vessels moved twice as fast, and images of Royce nude jumped into her mind.

She did the only thing she could.

She whimpered.

Royce lost all control.

That sound was so close to the sound she made right before she climaxed that he had to have her, at least a taste, something quick that would satisfy his craving, then let him put her from his mind. They couldn't be the same together as they had once been. It was too late for that, and he'd best prove it to both of them. He could lift her up, see her reaction, then step back.

He would tease her until she was so wet she would squirm with need, and then leave her. She would hate him for it. He'd dreamt of doing it many times, make her curse him the same way he had her, for the past twelve years.

Bring her to near completion, then leave her cold. Alone, frustrated, confused. All the things he'd gone through when he'd found out she was engaged to another. That's what he would do.

Unfortunately he looked into her eyes, the blue as deep as a sapphire. Not until he caught her gaze had he remembered how the color of her eyes would change. Sometimes the color of the sky, other times a need or fury could darken them to a color that mesmerized him. There was no way he could leave her now.

Not until he buried his face in the silky waves of her long dark brown tresses, tugged her close so her breasts pushed against him, close enough to feel her nipples harden. More than anything, he needed to feel her squirm against him, pushing her need against his erect member until he nearly exploded.

He lifted her up, his hands on her bottom, the rounded cheeks fitting his hands perfectly, just as they used to, and he pulled her toward him. He wanted her to feel his hardness against her woman's place, show her what she was missing. He could feel her need through the fabric of her skirts in how she trembled and pressed against him. He wished he had his hands on her skin to feel her heat coursing through her.

But he didn't dare. He had to keep control.

Had. To.

He moved her backwards, until she hit the wall, and he thrust his hips against her just as he would if he lifted her skirts. Then the worst happened.

She moaned. "Please, Royce. I need you."

Push her away, torture her. She deserves it.

But his thoughts were lost, the effect of being so close to her. Memories flooded his mind. Memories of their kissing, their many different ways of lovemaking, how she would tease him, sauntering over to him and with a mere touch set him off. She made a game of it, seeing how little it took to get him hard. Leaning over in a low-cut gown, whispering unladylike words in his ear, words of what she wished for him to do to her and she to him. But when she'd tease him with glimpses of her bare body—ah, that had the quickest effect of all. She had no idea how beautiful she was bare, her breasts standing proud and begging to be touched, caressed.

Licked. Suckled. Massaged until she cried out.

"Just once. Please." Tears rolled down her face. "I missed you so much. All these years, I've loved you."

He was powerless against her. He carried her through the doorway to the bedchamber, where they'd spent so many hours in days gone by, and tossed her down on the bed. He lifted her skirts and found his own hardness. He spread her legs to find her drenched with her own need, and want, need, desperation pulsed through him harder than any of her looks, teases, or words could make him feel.

Pausing at her entrance, he whispered, "Tell me ye want this as much as I do."

He gazed into her eyes, a small part of him wishing she'd refuse him. Of course, the traitorous member between his legs was begging for entrance, weeping with need.

Say it. Say ye want me. Please, Rhona. I need to hear it again.

He cursed himself, reminding himself of his plan, of what he'd thought of doing for years.

So I can pull away and leave ye aching with need.

"More. I dreamed of you last eve, of your lovemaking, of how well we fit together. No one but you fits me right, Royce. Please."

He nearly pulled away, jerked in his indecision, but then she moaned again, and he was lost in Rhona. He groaned and thrust ahead, burying himself deep inside her, so deep that she cried with pleasure, arching into his invasion, pushing back at him, trying to establish a rhythm with him.

He'd dreamed of this through many lonely nights. One more night wouldn't hurt. This would tell him exactly what he needed to know. He leaned down and ripped the ribbons of her bodice with his teeth, tearing the fabric of the gown and her chemise away enough that his tongue could touch her nipple. When he saw it had peaked already, he chuckled and took her areola in his mouth, suckling her until she cried out again.

He'd brought her to climax once just with his tongue on her breasts and a hand cupping her sex. Could he still do it?

Were they as good together as they used to be?

Rhona moaned, one hand gripping his hair at the back of his head and the other his backside, pulling him forward as her legs rose to invite him in deeper. Before he knew it, they rocked together in the same rhythm they'd always had, her moans driving him faster as she called his name.

"Royce, harder. Take me hard. Please."

He had no control. In days of old, he would tease her and hold his own climax until she finished, but he knew better than to think he could hold out this time. It had been too long since he'd been near her. Her scent, her sounds, her voice alone would drive him over the edge, and he wanted it. Wanted her with a desire so deep that it frightened him.

Now that he was inside her, all thoughts of leaving her unsatisfied vanished. He had to hear the quiet sounds she made, the hitch in her voice, the low guttural sounds as her pleasure climbed, the small whimper when she was losing control. He knew all those sounds.

Every one of them had replayed in his head over and over again since he'd lost her.

He did as she asked, and her nails dug into his upper arm, where her hand had slipped, and into his arse. The sharp pain ripped through him at the same time her climax took her, her moans telling him how strong her finish was, her contractions milking him until he shouted with a grunt, clamping his jaw closed to contain her name. That one effort took the last shred of his control, and he followed her over the edge.

His head dropped against her, but he managed to hold his weight on his elbows as he nuzzled her neck, kissing her once. They gasped in two different rhythms, her breathing coming harder than he'd ever heard it.

"Wait. Don't leave me yet." She whispered into his ear, "Please, two moments before you pull out."

He did as she asked and held himself there, his hardness shrinking but staying inside her. He knew if he waited a few more moments, he'd rouse all over again with a need that would drive him to a second round, but he couldn't allow it.

He slipped out and pushed away from her, settling her skirts out of respect. She rolled onto her side, her arm coming around her waist as if to hug herself. He found a stool by the hearth and plopped down on it, leaning forward with his elbows on his knees.

He waited until he controlled his breathing before he said, "I'm sorry. That shouldnae have happened."

A fury crossed her face, that temper of hers surfacing in a second. He'd always loved her temper. He hated women who said aye to everything and everyone, agreeing as if they had no mind or opinion of their own.

Rhona had a mind of her own, and she didn't fear making it known. "Sorry? Why? You enjoyed it as much as I did, and if you tell me otherwise, you'll be lying. I know you. I *know* you in ways no one else does. How can you share something so beautiful and then be in a hurry to finish it?"

He couldn't answer her, so he found a pitcher that somehow still had water in it and washed up a bit with a linen square, then brought a clean linen and the pitcher to her.

"I'm sorry, but I must go."

"But what about my proposal? Only we can stop this."

"We dinnae have that kind of power, Rhona. It was nice, but we cannae be."

"Why not?"

He turned to her when he reached the door, stopping. "Because I cannae ever forgive ye. Ye are the one who said aye at the altar to another."

He crossed the main room of the lodge quickly, before he could allow second thoughts to invade, and stepped into the fresh air. He closed the door behind him, hating to do it even as he walked away. That wee bit of lovemaking told him his feelings for her were still there and as strong as ever. But he would have to have all of her. Any less would rip out his heart.

She must have roused herself and followed. She called out from behind him, "Royce, please help end the feud. You're not a quitter!"

He never was, but everything was different now. Everything.

CHAPTER THREE

R HONA WANTED TO scream at the man. That pain in the arse was not going to get away with ignoring her, so she chased after him, not caring what her ripped bodice looked like. Let it serve as a reminder of how much he'd wanted her a short time ago.

"How dare you come and take what you want without listening to me." She caught up with him halfway across the clearing, grabbed his shoulder, and squeezed.

He spun around with that look on his face that could make his men take a step back, but she knew it well.

"I'm not afraid of you, Royce MacRob, so stop trying to intimidate me. It will not work. Why can you not stay and discuss this with me?"

"What is there to discuss? We coupled, we finished, now we go our separate ways. What more do ye wish from me? Did ye no' take enough of me when ye left?"

"Did you not hear a word I said? I want you to help me devise a way to stop the king from forcing any more marriages on our clans. He's forced two. Is that not enough for you?"

Her fisted hands settled on her hips as she leaned forward to speak with him.

Royce lowered his voice. "Rhona, I'll no' marry ye. Ye as good as cuckolded me, and I'll no' forgive ye. What else could the two of us possibly do to put an end to this? Ye have only a moment to explain before I take my leave."

"We could meet the king in Edinburgh. Mayhap on his own soil, he'll be more willing to listen to reason."

"We dinnae even know if he's in Edinburgh. I'll no' chase blindly after him when I'm needed here." His hands swung up over his head as he worked through his thoughts. "And why do ye talk like the bloody English when ye're a Scot through and through?"

"Because my husband insisted I speak like the English. He thought it would help him become a favorite of King Henry."

"Fine, talk as a false person does. 'Tis something to add to yer list of faults, woman."

"You're keeping lists on me?" She stepped closer so she could whisper to him. "I'll take that as a compliment. You must think of me often." She stepped back with a smirk.

He followed her, mirroring her step, then taking another, but she refused to let him intimidate her, holding her ground, though staring up at him gave her neck a crick.

His gaze narrowed as he stared down at her. "Dinnae think that ye occupy my mind much. Ye dinnae. Ye did once but nae more. I have better things to think about."

They glared at each other, neither one moving. His scent filled her nose, and she crossed her arms to hide the fact that her nipples had reacted so strongly to his closeness. "You are a pain in my arse, MacRob."

He leaned down to whisper to her, nearly nuzzling her neck. "But what am I to yer nipples? I know why ye crossed yer arms, lass. I recall how quickly ye always responded to my closeness. Naught has changed, has it?"

With a wicked grin, he stepped back, looking as if someone had just put a medal on his chest.

She gave him a shove. "We can at least search for Tor and Ainsley. She's my sister, and I love her. I cannot lose my only sibling."

"Ye have two siblings, ye wee fool," he said, taking a step closer. "One sister and one brother, yer laird."

"Nay, I don't. I used to have a brother, but he proved he did not love me, so I've declared him not my blood anymore."

"Och. He's yer laird and there's no denying it." Royce began to turn away but stopped halfway around, his gaze snagged on something.

She looked too, not surprised to see what had caught his attention. "Stop looking at the tree!"

Their tree. The tree they'd had fabulous sex against. Her back and backside had been sore for days. Her woman's parts had been singing for days.

"I'm no' looking at a tree. Why would I?"

"Because that's the tree you took me against. Or are you going to try to tell me you don't recall some of our best lovemaking?"

His eyes widened. "That tree? Nay—yer mind is playing tricks on ye. I'm leaving. I'll no' stay here to discuss some event ye created in yer mind."

He spun around and stalked away, not looking back.

"Royce, please consider my suggestions," she called out after him, but he ignored her. "My sister. Your brother. Are you not worried about them? No one has seen them for days!" She had to get through to him. She just had to make him listen.

Royce called out over his shoulder, "Goodbye, Rhona!"

She threw a rock at him and missed.

She hated him. How dare he forget about their tree sex!

Oh, how he hated the wench. She toyed with him the same way he had intended to toy with her.

Make her want him? Done. Remind her of the pleasure he could bring her? Done. He knew how good it had been for her by how long her contractions lasted. It would have taken no time at all to bring her to another climax, she was that close to a second one.

Leave her wanting more? Unfortunately, she'd done that to *him*. Many times he'd wished they could couple one more time so he would realize it hadn't been as good as he remembered. Then he wouldn't crave her quite so desperately. Their spark would be gone.

He surely was wrong about that. This day, he swore, had been better than any memory.

And now, with every breath he took, he wanted more of her.

"Hellfire," he said to himself.

He was the one wishing, wanting, not Rhona.

Mungo, his faithful second, stood at the edge of the forest. Royce gave him a grunt of acknowledgment, while Mungo smirked, waiting to see what he had to say, if he were to guess.

When he didn't offer anything, Mungo probed, "Ye look like a man who has just had his bollocks blown by intense pleasure but was sent away before he could go a second round."

Royce stopped in his tracks. "How the hell would ye guess that? I sure as hell dinnae look satisfied at all. Even though she did a fine job of it in round one."

He smirked at his closest confidant, moving his shoulder to feel the sting of the scratches Rhona had left.

"Yer yell carries, my friend." He winked. "A sound I've heard before, though 'tis been a long time since I've heard one with such lusty satisfaction."

He barked out a laugh at that comment. He'd been caught, and there was no use denying the truth. He moved on toward their horses.

"That good? Have ye the marks as proof?"

"Aye, in two places, if ye must know." He couldn't hide that he was pleased by that.

"Is that why she invited ye to yer old trysting spot?"

They mounted their horses and headed out, and he decided to wait until they were deeper into the trees before speaking his mind. Ears loved to wave in the wind, and the tongues followed, though he didn't think there would be anyone in this corner of MacRob land to hear.

When he felt it was safe, he said, "She wishes to marry me."

Mungo barked a laugh. "I didnae think Rhona was ever that foolish."

"She's no'. 'Tis for a reason."

"Which is?"

"She thinks if we marry, we could convince the king to end the forcing of marriages. If we marry, 'twould mark the end of the feud." He glanced over at Mungo, interested to hear what he thought of her proposal. "And I cannae doubt her reasoning. We are the reason for the feud, are we no'?"

"She could be right. But ye refused, I assume."

"Aye. She said we'd annul it later. I'm no' about to live with her and no' live like a married couple. 'Tis all or naught for me."

"So ye chose naught rather than take a chance by marrying the lass of yer dreams. The one ye've pined over for years. Take a chance and see if ye could convince her to join ye in yer bed every night."

"She didnae seem to be interested in such a proposal." He stared straight ahead, realizing that everything he was about to say would suggest he should agree to at least help her.

Mungo didn't let up on him. "But ye had some fun in her bed? How much convincing did that take? Did ye have to beg her?"

He stopped his horse and turned to face Mungo, to make sure his friend caught him rolling his eyes. "Truly ye ask me that question?"

"I didnae think ye would have offered, knowing how ye feel. So what exactly happened?"

He pulled on the reins of his horse, moving forward again. "I dunno. Just happened. I planned to tease her as I've always wished to do, but I took it too far. Thought I could stop, but . . . we were too close . . . her scent." That was all he would admit. There was a part of him still a gentleman, not willing to admit he knew the scent of her need.

"She still has a hold on yer heart. No' surprised at all. So 'tis all she wanted? For ye to marry her?"

He wanted to glare at the man for knowing him too well, but instead, he let out a deep sigh. "Nay, she suggested we could go together and seek out the king. Ask him to end the forced marriages. She also suggested we look for Tor and Ainsley."

Mungo shrugged and gave him a look. One he knew exactly.

"I know. She does have a good point. Mayhap now that I'm away and thinking clearly, I'll reconsider. We could go to the king and search for Tor. 'Twould no' be a long trip to Edinburgh."

"Let it go until ye are sure ye are thinking with yer head and no' yer cock. It tends to get in the way of sound thinking."

He surely could not argue with Mungo's reasoning.

They arrived at Castle MacRob and headed to the stables.

"Any news?" Royce asked the stable lad who came to get their horses.

"Nay, naught about Tor."

He headed straight for his solar, going through the postern door, moving quickly so he wouldn't have to speak to anyone. The MacRob keep had an entrance to the back, so he did not need to go through the main door or central hall. Mungo followed, speaking to all those Royce ignored. Once inside, Royce spoke to Effie, whose duty was to wait upon him in his solar, telling her to bring him an ale and a meat pie, then he headed to his desk.

Effie returned quickly with their food, then left them alone.

Royce looked at the man who was more friend than second-in-command. They were close enough to be brothers, though their opposite appearances would reveal the truth. Mungo's hair was dark red and had so much curl to it that he looked like a wild man at times. He'd always complained it was impossible to get a comb through it. He worked hard in the lists and had arms like tree trunks, one no one would like to have to fight against. "What would ye do?"

Mungo thought for a moment, tapping the arm of his chair, then said, "I think ye should go with her to Edinburgh. Ye claim that ye are over her, but we both know the truth. No one can ever replace her. She is the reason ye've never married. She is the reason ye argued with yer sire. She is the reason ye have no bairns, no heirs to the lairdship. Ye only have the one brother left, and his marriage seems unlikely to be fruitful. I highly doubt Tor could handle the lairdship anyway. He's too irresponsible. And since he hates his wife, I dinnae think they would do well running the clan."

"He may change. I think he will be responsible eventually. He's young yet."

"I beg yer pardon, Laird, but yer brother doesnae know the name of yer priest, if it were my guess. He doesnae have the makings of a true leader, one who knows all that takes place in the clan. Ye know 'tis true and ye know of what I speak." Mungo tipped his head and gave him the look that told him how serious he was.

"I know my brother is taken by the light-skirts in the clan." He couldn't help but smirk when thinking of Tor and his lusty desires.

"And he'll toss any skirt he can from here to Berwick. Wait until his new wife catches him. She'll slice a bollock in two in his sleep."

Royce couldn't stop the laughter from bursting out of his chest. "Tor will mend his ways. I'm sure of it."

"Forget about Tor, this is about ye. What matters is that Rhona Shaw has had a major effect on every part of yer life. She was the key to yer happiness. I think 'tis worth it to spend more time with the woman to see if ye suit. Is there aught there after all these years?"

"I doubt it." That was a lie—he'd seen for himself that something persisted between them. And he knew her MacAdder husband had never won her esteem.

"But ye need to know that for certes. If ye feel it in yer bones, if ye can spend time with her and know ye no longer fit each other, mayhap ye can finally seek a woman to stand at yer side. As it is, she is the reason ye havenae moved on. She's the key to yer happiness, whether ye wish to admit it or no'."

"Mayhap I am over her. Did ye consider that possibility?" He leaned forward and slammed his palms down on the desk.

"Aye, but based on the look on yer face when ye came out of that lodge, and the roar I heard when ye gave her yer seed, I'd say ye are far from over her. Mayhap spending more time with her is the way to get over her. She's changed and so have ye."

Royce stared at the wall behind Mungo. He made good points, and Royce could not argue any of them.

"And ye've forgotten the best reason for going with her, wherever ye choose to go. Where the hell is yer brother? And if ye dinnae find Ian and Marta, two more will be forced to marry. 'Tis wrong. And we have nae idea who it would be. He could force the two of ye to marry, or have ye no' thought of that possibility?"

Royce drummed his fingers on the desk, considering his options. "Ye are correct. I'll go to her on the morrow and arrange a journey to

Edinburgh."

"Why no' return this day?"

"'Tis too late in the day. Besides, I must take care of another issue before I see Rhona again." It would not be a pleasant conversation, but this situation with Rhona was forcing him to take a step he should have taken long ago.

He had to end his relationship with Louisa.

CHAPTER FOUR

RHONA RETURNED TO her small hut located on the outskirts of Shaw land, moving carefully through the dark forest. She carried a lantern, which she thought only made the shadows more startling than if she walked in the dark.

Her maid Forsy had stayed with her during her marriage and brought her to this hut shortly after she gave birth to Annie, who was now five summers old.

Annie was the light of her life and the reason she'd made her escape from Duncan MacAdder's castle. The marriage had been miserable from the start, but his actions after she gave birth to Annie had driven home the necessity of fleeing. She could not raise a child in that place.

MacAdder had beaten her so badly that she could barely see her beautiful newborn daughter through her swollen eyelids. The devil had blamed her for delivering a lass instead of a lad. And he'd done it in the great hall in front of everyone.

"You did this apurpose to embarrass me, I'm sure of it." The hatred in his eyes had spoken louder than any words or insults he might have hurled at her. "I need an heir, and you'll give me one. You get a sennight before we make another. And this time, it better be a lad."

She'd fought back at first, and one swing of her fist had connected with his face. After that humiliation, he had two men hold her down so he could "beat her properly." They'd locked her away, alone and nearly dead, in a bare bedchamber. Forsy had been sent in to attend to her the next day. As soon as her dear companion had seen her, she'd promised to get her away.

"Dinnae worry about your wee lassie. She's safe away already." She'd taken the bairn to her brother Giric and told him what had happened to Rhona.

Forsy had fed Rhona some broth and bathed her carefully, and as a guard came to usher her away, Forsy had whispered, "I'll be back this eve. Late. Say naught."

"Don't worry." She'd known there'd be no one to tell. Her husband would not see her until she was strong enough to be beaten again or taken to his bed. Forsy had left, a new look of determination on her face.

Forsy had returned that night and managed to get Rhona to her feet, but she almost crumpled to the floor. "Hurts too much. I can't do it. Please leave me to die."

"I willnae," her rescuer had whispered in her ear. "Ye have a wee daughter at a cottage on Shaw land. My brother Giric has found a small hut in the forest and has fixed it for us. I'll no' let this evil man kill ye. So get up for yer daughter,

Rhona. Yer husband is deep in his cups, and we must go while we have the chance."

Together they'd hobbled down the back staircase to where Giric awaited them. He'd lifted her and carried her away into the night. An oxcart awaited them, piled high with straw, and she'd nestled into the warmth. Forsy, an old shawl over her head, drove, and Giric rode his own horse ahead, watching for trouble. They'd come away with only what meager belongings would fit in a small, easy-to-carry bag.

The windows of the small cottage glowed with more warmth than Rhona had felt in years, and she found she could walk inside more easily than when she'd left her MacAdder prison. She broke into sobs when she saw her dear sister, Ainsley, trying to feed her infant daughter some goat's milk, using a cloth fastened over the end of a cow's horn that the babe might suck on. She hadn't seen Ainsley since her wedding day.

Her husband had found her about a fortnight later, banging on the door and demanding she return. She'd stood tall and told him that if he ever touched her again, she'd go to her brother and the MacRobs and tell them exactly what he had done to her.

Everyone feared Royce MacRob, and she had to hope MacAdder did also. The ploy had worked. She'd never seen her husband again, though she felt bad for his mistresses, upon whom he'd take out his anger.

She'd lived hidden away with her daughter for nearly five years, her only companions Forsy and

Ainsley, who visited regularly. Giric had done the heavy work, bringing wood and food when he'd gone hunting, but she'd learned to hunt for them too and had grown strong from doing the work the cottage required, making repairs, tending the garden, caring for their milk goat. It had given her purpose. Aye, it had been lonely, but far better than living with Duncan.

Now the bastard was dead. She could have taken Annie back—the inheritance was hers, as Duncan's only child—but she had no desire to return to that place. Duncan's brother and his second had been the two who held her for that final beating, and she'd spit on both of them if she ever saw them again. And her daughter was too young for such a burden anyway. If anything remained of the clan when she came of age, perhaps then she could claim her birthright.

She opened the cottage door and stuck her head in. The warmth of the place made her heart glow with pleasure and pride. "Who is here that I love more than any other?"

"Mama! Surely it must be me. You love me more than any other." Her dark-haired daughter, her hair the exact color as her own, her eyes bluer than the sky on a glorious day, sat on a stool at the table, cutting apples with a dull knife they'd found for her to use. She hopped off her stool to give her mother a hug. "I missed you, Mama."

"I was not gone that long." She glanced at the table. "Someone harvested today. You have carrots and turnips."

"And parsnips. We'll use them on the morrow.

And Forsy found apples ripening early on a tree. Four of them for our evening meal."

Forsy tousled Annie's hair. "And the Shaw cook sent a bone from a pig for our vegetable stew, so we'll have more flavor. I put it in a while ago. We'll eat fine this week."

"Annie, do Mama a favor and go to the stream for a bucket of water. Do not dawdle, just hurry back."

Once she was gone, Forsy's questions began.

"Ye must have something good to tell me. The man ye loved? Royce MacRob—did ye see him?"

"Aye." She moved to the hearth and rubbed her hands together in the warmth coming from the fire.

"Has he changed much?"

She hadn't thought of that right away, but now she did, thinking of every part of his face, his hands.

"Nay, he has not changed a bit. Still as handsome as ever." She stared into the flames, remembering how wonderful it had been to be in his arms.

"Did he agree to yer proposal?"

"Nay. He refused to marry me, because he said he'll never forgive me for what I'd done. And I suggested going after my sister and his brother, and seeking an audience with the king. He rejected it all."

"The man wasnae agreeable? Although he was agreeable enough to tear yer ribbons, I see."

A deep sigh escaped. "He was not agreeable to my proposal."

She quickly changed her gown before her

daughter could notice her disarray now that she
had removed her cloak.

She stared at her hands, tears misting her gaze.
How wonderful it had been to be near him, feel
his skin, gaze into his eyes. She was quite certain
he would have nothing kind to say about her,
despite it all.

"Forsy, do not get your hopes up. We will never
marry. He'll never be more than a pain in my
arse."

Forsy shook her head, making the odd clicking
sound that meant she was passing judgment.

"Why do you click so?"

Forsy's head jerked up as if she hadn't realized
she'd made the noise. "Because ye and Royce
were a match meant to be. 'Tis such a shame that
neither of ye can see it the way the rest of us do.
I understand the issue with MacAdder, but now
he is gone. Tell yer brother he has no say in yer
next marriage."

"I wish it were that simple. I offered, but Royce
refused—it is he himself, not my brother, who
has stopped it. It is no longer a possibility."

"Do ye think that 'tis time for ye to mend yer
grievance with yer brother? If no' for yerself,
then for yer daughter. The lass is growing up, and
she deserves to know the others in her clan. She
should know her uncle and the others. Ainsley
has been wonderful for her. Please give it thought,
Rhona. Forgive me if I overstep my boundaries,
but I have watched this wee lassie for so long, and
she needs a friend. One her own age."

Rhona plopped into a chair in front of the

hearth, staring into the flames. Forsy was right.
She wouldn't go to her brother if not for wee
Annie, but the lassie did deserve a friend. She'd
already attempted to befriend every animal that
crossed her path. And Rhona needed to know
that Broden would care for Annie if anything
happened to her. She only had Ainsley . . . and
Broden, if she willed it.

Perhaps it was time to have a talk with her
brother.

~

Royce pulled his horse to a halt at the Shaw
stables, and a lad hurried out to take charge of
his mount.

"My lord, are ye here to stay?"

"Aye, for a bit. Ye may brush him down and
feed him some oats. I gave him a good run on
the way here."

"Aye, my lord. I'll take good care of him." The
lad took the reins from him.

As Royce stepped away from the stables, Giric,
the Shaw laird's second, came around the corner.
"The laird of the MacRobs cannae enter without
being seen by many. What is yer purpose, Royce?"

They were polite to each other, thanks to the
king's interference and the supposedly peaceful
stance between the families. Royce's sister Catlin's
marriage to the laird of the Shaws had enforced
their begrudging truce. But everyone knew that
under the polite words, anger and resentment still
surged.

"I came to visit my sister, Giric. Is that no'

allowed? And I'll see her husband as long as I'm here. I'm anxious to hear about any progress in finding Ian and Marta."

"If we knew something, we would tell ye." Giric planted his feet apart and put his hand on the hilt of his sword.

"Take yer blasted hand from yer weapon or prepare to fight me." Royce knew his sword skills were unparalleled. If he needed to fight anyone, it would be the laird, not his second. He narrowed his eyes as he waited for Giric to move his hand, which he did only slowly.

"Ye insult us. We'd never keep information from ye or lie to ye about the search. We're an honorable clan."

"Where is my sister?" He would not be waylaid from his purpose. First, he had to see if Catlin fared well in the keep of the enemy, husband or not. Then he would see what Shaw had heard about Ian and Marta. He would visit Louisa on his way home.

Now that he'd seen Rhona again, he couldn't get her out of his mind.

Louisa lived in a cottage not far from Rhona's cottage. He usually visited her place at night, and it was set far away from the other huts and nestled in a cluster of trees. It had taken some time and effort to find her a safe place to live and receive him, but he would not have it widely known that his mistress was a Shaw.

Louisa kept mum about their relationship and the arrangement—she would face dire consequences if they were found out, more

than him, even. He gave her enough c
wouldn't have to serve in the laird'
she took care of his needs. Her other pur
one he only trusted to her.

She spied on Rhona and let him know how she and her daughter fared. Rumors had abounded about her husband's feelings about their newborn bairn, so he'd made sure to follow up on her well-being as soon as word reached him. If he hadn't known where she'd taken refuge from MacAdder, he would have been beside himself with worry. But this way, he was always aware of her location and her practices.

And any men she entertained. Though to his knowledge, she'd never slept with another since her husband had punished her for bearing a lass. Or so it was said.

Cruel bastard.

He recalled the day he'd learned MacAdder had beaten her after she birthed his child. He'd waited until the bastard had snuck out of his castle to rendezvous with one of his mistresses, then came up behind him and knocked him off his horse. The fool traveled with no guards, which made his work easy.

Then he'd beaten him worse than MacAdder had beaten Rhona.

He should have killed him.

He couldn't help but smile over that one. Giric gave him an odd look, but he said, "My sister? Will ye no' take me to her?"

"Aye, she's in the hall with my laird." He led the way to the hall, a separate building from the keep. Royce had been more surprised than anyone when Catlin had admitted she'd fallen for Broden Shaw, but after seeing the two together, he could see it was a good match. He hated the man for what he'd done to him and Rhona, but he appeared to truly love Catlin.

Royce stepped inside the hall and gave his eyes a moment to adjust to the light.

His sister called out to him. "Royce! My goodness! I'm so happy to see ye. Please come in."

She spoke to one of the serving lasses and sent her off for food and ale for him.

He greeted Catlin with a kiss to her cheek and a swift hug, making sure to squeeze her enough to test for bruises anywhere on her. If the bastard dared to ever take a fist to his sister, it would be the last thing he ever did.

Clever Catlin murmured low, "Nay, he doesnae beat me, Royce. I know the purpose of yer tight squeeze."

He didn't try to hide his smirk but rubbed her upper arm. "Ye are happy, sister?"

"Aye, verra happy. Only one thing sullies my happiness."

"And what would that be? Tell me and I'll fix it, if 'tis in my power."

"I continue my work on this puzzle involving Ian and Marta."

Broden stood to greet him, taking his wife's hand and tugging her close. "MacRob, welcome to our home."

He couldn't help but arch his brow at the word

"welcome." For many years he had not been welcome here. He reminded himself that it was this man's doing and his alone that had kept Royce and Rhona apart.

"Have ye come to see what good care I take of yer sister?" He motioned for Royce to take a seat in front of the hearth while he settled Catlin in a chair next to her brother.

"If only I could have taken such care of yers, but I have other business tonight." He wouldn't cause trouble, but he had to mention Shaw's biggest failure as laird. It had been his first major decision as head of his family and clan. What a bungle he'd made of it. If not for this man, many lives would have been different, and they wouldn't be in this mess now.

"What's yer business, then?" Shaw crossed his arms where he stood next to the hearth.

"What have ye learned new of Ian and Marta?"

"Naught since the wedding and that healer's tale. Ye?"

"Naught. What about Ainsley and Tor?"

Shaw dropped his gaze to the floor, his hand running down the back of his head to his neck. "Naught. I'll admit to being worried. We should have heard something from them by now." He lifted his head to lock eyes with Royce. "My greatest worry is that Ainsley will try to kill Tor while he's sleeping."

"I am also concerned. My brother would never hurt a lass—perhaps he has more kindness than yer sister. My fear is he left her at a kirk somewhere. I know their personalities will clash."

He sighed and glanced at his sister. "'Twas cruelly done by our king."

"'Tis unwise for ye to say so," Shaw reminded him.

"Have the king come for me. After word gets about of what he's done to our two clans, his reputation will be broken, and King Henry will be rejoicing."

His sister stood up. "Enough. I love both of ye, and ye are ripping my heart in two. All ye do is talk and accuse each other's clans of the worst evil. Can we no' work in concert to solve this problem for four people we all love?"

"*Two* people I love," Royce clarified. "I dinnae care for Ainsley or Ian."

"Royce!" Then his dear sister stomped her foot. She must be angry—he'd never seen her do that before.

"Fine. I'll be kind. Any suggestions, Shaw?"

"Nay. Ye?"

"I have had one suggestion brought to me, and I am considering it."

"What is it?" Shaw asked.

"I met with Rhona, and she has asked me to travel with her to Edinburgh for an audience with the king. She thinks if we go together, we can persuade him to end this daft plan of his. We could search for Tor and Ainsley along the way."

Shaw's eyes widened in outrage. "I hope she turned ye down. Ye know I'd no' approve of Rhona doing aught with ye."

"Broden!" Catlin exclaimed.

"'Twas her idea, Shaw. Ye still cannae accept

that we would be great together, can ye?" He lunged to his feet and moved closer until he was nose-to-nose with Broden. "Ye are a fool. She's a widow now, and ye've little authority over her, anyway."

Catlin said, "Broden, please reconsider. I think 'tis a good plan. We willnae find Tor and Ainsley or Ian and Marta by just sitting here."

"Nay. I'm sorry, love, but I've already lost Ainsley, and ye are asking me to risk Rhona as well, though she hasnae spoken to me in years. And I know no' if Ainsley will ever return. I'll no' lose them both."

"Yer objections are noted, Shaw, for what little they're worth." Royce stepped back, leaned down to kiss his sister on the cheek again. "It pleases me to see ye happy with yer new husband, but I'll take my leave now."

He strode back across the hall to the door, stopping to turn around to look at the two still by the fire. Catlin had moved next to her husband and clasped his hand, her expression one of concern.

He looked at Shaw and said, "Ye just made my mind up, Shaw. Rhona and I'll be traveling together."

"The hell ye will."

Royce grinned and waved. "See ye when we return."

CHAPTER FIVE

ROYCE WALKED OUT of that meeting smiling, not because he'd learned anything new or that he was going to speak with Rhona again, but because it had felt so good to defy the bastard.

As if he were going to allow Broden Shaw to tell him what to do.

He'd go see Rhona on the morrow, but first, Louisa.

This would not be a good visit, but it was essential. He could not be close to Rhona if he was seeing Louisa. He did have some morals.

If his father could see him now, would he be proud?

Right before his sire passed away, Royce had argued with him about his future. His father had insisted he marry another, since Rhona was married and gone to MacAdder.

"Ye must marry. As my heir, 'tis yer moral and legal obligation to have sons to pass this castle down to so our land stays MacRob land. All of our grandsires would roll in their graves if the land went to another. Ye must have at least two heirs, and ye cannae do that without a wife." His father had stood tall, hadn't looked like he was ill at all, yet he'd died the very next day.

"Da, I'll no' marry another. Rhona is the only one for me. Adair and Tor can have bairns. Mayhap he'll have five lads to make ye happy. And Catlin will have sons, too, in case my brothers have none. The land could go to her sons, or her daughter if 'tis all she has. Catlin is a verra smart lass, and her bairns will be smart and talented too." He couldn't have predicted they would lose Adair before he married.

His father hadn't agreed with anything he'd said, instead surprising him with how much and how little he had known about his relationship with Rhona. "Ah, lad. Ye've got it all wrong. So ye lay with the lass, and ye like her. There are many other lasses who'll be fine in yer bed. 'Tis no' the only thing there is in a marriage."

Royce could feel his eyes widen and the blush start at his neck and move upward. How the hell had the old man figured out he'd bedded Rhona? But at the same time, his father seemed to have no idea of how well they matched out of bed, as well. It was more than *liking* between them.

"Ye think I didnae know ye've bedded her? The two of ye could awaken every soul in the graveyards on MacRob land. 'Tis probably better ye dinnae marry her. 'Twould no' be seemly to have the entire clan hear their lord and lady carry on so."

Royce mumbled, "But we were in the hunting lodge, far enough away . . ."

"Never ye mind. Ye'll do as I say. Ye have a

fortnight to get over yer loss, but then ye'll be finding another. There are many lasses to choose from. Pick her sister, if ye like. But Shaw probably wouldnae accept ye for her either." His father had waved his hand at him and said, "I have to go lie down. I'm tired. I dinnae understand why the least bit I do tires me of late. I'll do as yer mother tells me. If I'm tired, I'll rest, so off I go."

Those were the last words he'd had with his father.

He looked up at the gray sky and mumbled, "Ye're probably no' too proud of me, Da. Before I'm done, I'll make ye proud, I swear it."

He turned off the main road between the Shaw and MacRob lands and onto the back path he'd cut long ago through the woods. Making his way there, he considered how best to approach Louisa with his news. Probably smart to break it off from the start. He couldn't stop himself from meandering closer to Rhona's cottage, even though it was a little distance from Louisa's. It was time for the evening meal, so he didn't expect to run into anyone.

He came through the trees, surprised to see a wee lassie tipping a jug into the water. The vessel was apparently heavy enough that she struggled with it. The lass had to be Rhona's daughter, Annie.

He came up next to her and asked, "May I be of assistance?"

"Aye." She quickly handed the container over to him and said, "I cannot hold it properly in the water. Usually I go to the burn near the waterfall, but I must move quickly this day."

He filled the jug and set it down at her feet, mostly because she was giving him an odd stare. When he looked directly at her, it was as if he were punched in the gut. The lass was the image of her mother, with blue eyes that looked like the sky on a summer morning. This had to be how Rhona looked as a bairn, the dark wavy hair the same color but tied back in a loose plait.

"I'll no' hurt ye, lass. Would ye like me to carry it to yer cottage?"

She gave him a puzzled look. "You sound like Giric. And you wear your gown too short like he does. You must be a man." She pointed to his legs. "And those are much hairier than Mama's. I've never seen Giric's legs up close, though."

He knelt down and said, "I'm guessing ye havenae seen many men. There are lads and there are lasses. Ye are a lass, and I was a lad until I grew big enough to be a man. Have ye never met yer sire?"

"My sire died before I could meet him. I have seen men on their horses when we go hunting, but she will not allow me to talk to them." She looked him over carefully again, so he didn't move, giving her the time she needed to absorb what she'd learned. "My thanks for helping me, but I must go now. I hope you'll be my friend."

"Of course I will. Shall I carry it for ye?"

She struggled, but that same look of perseverance and plain grit crossed her face, much the same as her mother often wore. "Good day to you, my lord."

Annie left without another word. He could easily love the lass and treat her as his own. He loved bairns, had once thought of having many with Rhona. But it was not to be.

He pushed himself to his feet and moved on, though he'd have watched the lass forever. Why hadn't he ever seen her before in the woods? When he gave it more thought, he realized that he'd only been here after dark.

His visits had always been well after the evening meal. Had he known what he'd been missing, he may have come earlier on occasion.

He sighed, forcing his feet away from the woman he adored and toward the one who had been little more than a convenience. Sweet as Louisa was, he'd never developed any true feelings for the woman.

Not when his heart was sewn up tight waiting for Rhona Shaw.

He knocked on the door lightly and let himself in.

Louisa stepped out of the back bedchamber, her eyes wide. "Royce, what brings ye here during the day, may I ask?"

"Greetings, Louisa. Am I interrupting aught? I wished to speak with ye."

A man appeared behind her in the bedchamber doorway. Royce didn't know him, but he wore a Shaw plaid and carried himself with the confidence and ease of a member of the guards.

"Who is bothering ye, love?" The glower on the guard's face told Royce what he needed to know. They were lovers.

A fury built inside him, but he forced himself to tamp it down. He had no way of knowing whether Louisa had informed this other man of their relationship, so he vowed to enter into the conversation as calm as he could. "My apologies. I didnae know ye had company. I'll take my leave."

"What did ye want, my lord? Could ye return later to tell me what yer problem is, if ye please?"

Her lover's hand wrapped around her waist protectively, and she did her best to push it aside but failed.

"'Tis no' important. I'll be off to Edinburgh soon, so I cannae return. Good day to ye both."

He spun around and left, closing the door behind him. This would prevent the scene he'd dreaded when Louisa learned he was cutting things off. Now he could let it go. In truth, he should be relieved. After all, she seemed happy with the man. If he treated her kindly, then mayhap they'd marry someday. He'd never demanded that she stay true to him. He only visited twice a month, and the woman had her own needs for companionship.

Or more coin.

Stop with yer suspicions. A man to protect her when ye're no' around is a good thing for any woman.

He could not ignore the coincidence, though. Another female in his life who ended up with another man.

Since ye have no plans to marry her, be glad! Ye need no' explain why ye're leaving.

She followed him out the door, closing it behind her so they were alone.

"Please, my lord. Forgive me. I havenae seen ye in a while."

She looked astonishingly contrite and vulnerable. He kept his voice low. "'Tis no concern of mine, Louisa. I never asked ye to shun other men, so 'tis to be expected. I came to tell ye I'm off to Edinburgh, and I know no' when I'll be returning. I willnae be back to see ye, even after I return. Ye dinnae need to check on Rhona. I'll end that task."

At first she looked unaffected by his comments, but when he mentioned Rhona, she started with surprise. "Where is Rhona going? Is she going with ye?"

"Possibly. I go to our king to discuss this feud. We must end it. Whether she chooses to join me in this endeavor is up to her. Good day, Louisa. I wish ye all the best with yer man there."

CHAPTER SIX

RHONA HEADED TOWARD the keep, waiting until Annie was in bed before going to speak with her brother. Forsy was right. It was time for her to end this hatred she held for her brother and move on. They needed to come together to find Ainsley.

It was dark and damp, and she tugged her mantle tight around her shoulders, her hood over her head. When she approached the gate on her way to the keep, she lifted her head and moved her hood back a wee bit. A guard she didn't recognize called out to her.

"Who are ye?"

"I'm here to see my brother," she drawled, frustrated because, as the elder sister of the laird, she shouldn't have to identify herself.

"Yer name?" he asked.

"Your laird's sister, Rhona," she barked at him.

He stepped away from the gates to greet her. "Truly, 'tis ye, Rhona? I've no' seen ye in years."

Now that he was closer, she recognized his voice, though he had changed quite a bit. "Hugh, it is me. I've been in hiding for a short time."

"But yer husband is dead. Why hide from yer

own brother?" His beard had turned gray and the hair on his head was much sparser than she recalled. "I always wondered why ye didnae return, but I didnae dare to ask. I know how yer brother is about ye, Rhona. But ye shouldnae avoid him. Why would ye stay away now?"

"Because I still hate him. Now, may I proceed or not? I didn't expect to be stopped on my way to the keep."

"Of course, my lady. Ye missed Royce. He was here earlier today." Hugh smiled, revealing a gap in his teeth he hadn't had last she'd seen him.

"Why would I care anything about Royce?" She tipped her head to the side in question. Perhaps she'd been away from others for too long and had forgotten how to be polite.

He lost his smile in an instant. "Yer pardon, my lady. I didnae mean aught by it. Please enter. I'll escort ye to the hall."

"Never mind, Hugh. I thank you, but I recall my way in. No hard feelings."

"Of course, my lady. If ye need aught, I'm here for ye." He nodded his head as if to make sure she believed him.

"Many thanks." She spun on her heel and headed inside. She didn't see many people about in the courtyard, but the ones she did see gave her odd looks. It was time for her to decide exactly how she would handle herself with her clanmates. She was back amongst her clan, and they hadn't seen her for years. They had probably heard tales, but no doubt many were inaccurate, exaggerated, or just plain lies.

She'd been gone for twelve years.

That realization made her think about her relationship with Royce. They'd been so young when they'd been together. After their short courtship, she thought they would live their entire lives together, forever happy, forever naïve.

So much had happened that she had to wipe the tears from her eyes and shove the thoughts away. If she didn't they'd drench her cheeks. She would not cry in front of her brother. How long had it been since she'd seen him up close?

There had been a day she'd loved her brother as much as a sister could, but after Broden became laird and acceded to MacAdder's pressure, ending her relationship with Royce, that love had turned to hate in equal measure. She hadn't spoken to him since.

Even when Royce's brother Adair had died two years ago, her family had not attended the funeral because of the feud.

She could not stand by Royce's side, though she should have been there because she'd loved Adair. Instead, she'd gone to Adair's grave on her own to give herself the chance to grieve privately. Adair had been so full of life, and she'd missed his last few years.

Being forced to live with MacAdder and then hiding from him had isolated her so much that stepping back into the world made her uncomfortable. But desperate times now forced her to take the steps she'd been avoiding for too long. Her dear sister was missing.

Ainsley had spent much time in her cottage

with them, especially when Annie had been a wee bairn. Rhona would never forget Ainsley's look of wonder and joy at the beauty of a wee bairn. And her companionship over the last few years had been a precious gift.

Rhona couldn't bear to lose her. She had to do something. Royce had lost one brother already. Why wasn't he more concerned about the only brother he had left?

She was going after Ainsley, no matter who approved or who went with her.

She stepped inside the hall and stopped, her gaze moving around the large area. The chatelaine, Hilda, was chatting quietly with the serving lasses about the next day's meals, and her brother and his new wife, Catlin, sat in front of the hearth while a few guards finished eating at the trestle tables.

When she stepped out from the shadows and closed the door behind her, all talking ceased and a hush fell over the hall. Hilda gave the lasses a push and they exited, heading toward the kitchens.

Rhona turned toward her brother and lifted her chin, daring him to argue with her. "I'd like a moment of your time, Broden."

Broden stood and nodded to her, motioned for everyone but Catlin to leave the hall, and the few remaining guards hurried out, looks of shock on their faces. She swallowed hard, trying her best to sort out her words which had been in her mind but unsaid for so long.

The hatred, the sorrow, the anger, the regret.

If only things had been different.

But if they had, she'd never have the light of her life, her sweet Annie.

She couldn't help but study her brother and his new wife. They made a striking couple. Catlin had grown into a beautiful woman, her hair a glossy brown swept back from her brow, her eyes the same shade of green as Royce's. Her brother's brow had a few furrows in it, but he was still a striking man, his hair dark and still long, but carefully trimmed. But what caught her most was the look in his gaze when he looked at his wife.

He adored Catlin.

Broden kissed his wife briefly on the lips and whispered in her ear. She moved away, and Giric, who'd just stepped into the hall behind her, led Catlin away, presumably to the keep and the laird's bedchamber, a separate building on Shaw land.

Rhona couldn't stop herself from speaking to Catlin as she passed. "Welcome to the clan."

Catlin stopped and leaned over to give her a quick hug but said nothing. They'd been playmates when they'd been younger, despite the age difference.

Once they were alone, her brother motioned for her to take a seat by the hearth. Instead she stopped in front of him. She opened her mouth to speak, but he held his hands up to stop her.

"Please. I have something I must say first."

She nodded and sat down, her brother handing her a fur for her lap. He didn't sit, instead paced to the fire and back before turning back to her. "I need to beg yer forgiveness for approving a marriage with Duncan MacAdder. Had I known his cruelty, I never would have allowed the wedding. I learned how he treated ye, though I didnae learn soon enough, and I am sorry for that. I deserve whatever condemnation ye've come to lay upon me."

Rhona stared at him in shock. Her brother's heartfelt apology threw her off, simply because she hadn't expected it. "Why did you wait so long to tell me?"

"I dinnae know. Pride, I suppose. I needed to know ye wished for any kind of reunion, that ye might hear the words if I spoke them. Mayhap my wedding to Catlin has given me a different view of everything."

Rhona forgot all her well-planned words. The ones she wished to fling at him just didn't come, replaced by something more important from a hidden place in her heart. "I have a daughter, Annie, who is now five summers old. It is time to bring her to her clan. She knows little of men, knows only that her father has passed away. She's had no playmates, and that should change. I've cheated her of many loving relationships, and I hope you will welcome her as your niece."

"Of course I will. I'm sure I will love her as I do all my siblings, even though I may no' agree with them. Ye are welcome to any chambers in the keep for ye and yer bairn. I'm hoping ye will return to take yer rightful place as the laird's eldest sister."

"In time. I wish to bring Annie here to meet you and Catlin, find a playmate for her, and let her grow accustomed to the castle and her family before we move in."

Her brother smirked.

"What is amusing?"

"First allow me to say ye are still the same beauty ye always were, Rhona. But ye lost yer Scot's tongue. Why?"

She sighed deeply. She hadn't attempted to change back, but in her heart she was a true Scot. "It was forced on me by my husband. Every time I used a Scottish burr I was quickly chastised. A quick slap or a stick across my knuckles taught me to do as he said." She couldn't stop herself from rubbing her knuckles, an old habit. One finger had scarred badly from his punishments, and the ridge of the old wound was both pain and comfort under her fingers. "He had the carpenter make the stick for him special, with sharp points chiseled along it. He carried it with him everywhere. While I try to rid my mind of everything that was Duncan MacAdder, it is harder to remove the scars."

Broden fell into a chair and hung his head for a long moment, then lifted his gaze to hers. "I am sorry for all ye endured. Ye and yer daughter are welcome always."

"My thanks to you. I have a more immediate concern tonight. Ainsley. What have you heard about Ainsley and Tor? I miss her terribly, am worried sick about their marriage, and I wish she would return." She fumbled with the soft fur in her lap. She felt so awkward in this conversation with the brother she'd hated for so long. Being this close to him, she couldn't help but notice that he had indeed aged. He looked much like their father, and that warmed her heart. If she could just truly understand why he had given in to MacAdder's demand for a betrothal when their sire hadn't been here.

"We have heard naught. Royce was here today, and he's no' heard aught from Tor either. I'm considering sending another patrol out for them, though I've sent several with no luck." He leaned back in his chair and crossed his legs, drumming his fingertips on the arm of the chair. "I dinnae like this."

"Speaking of Royce, I have suggested we make a trip together to see King Alexander ourselves. I will come out of hiding for my sister and because I hope to prevent any more of the horrid matches he's making. Though it worked out for the best in your case, I don't think it will for Ainsley, and who knows for certain who he will choose next?"

Broden bolted out of his chair and began to pace again. He stopped abruptly in front of her. "Royce informed me of yer suggestion. I forbid it."

She stood up, her hands going to her hips. "You forbid what exactly?"

"I forbid ye to have aught to do with Royce."

"You just apologized for not allowing our marriage and forcing me to marry Duncan MacAdder. What the hell, Broden? What possible objection to Royce can you have?"

"I apologized for forcing ye to marry the beast ye did. But Royce changed over the years. He will toy with yer feelings, in my opinion. Yer marriage to MacAdder hardened him." His eyes blazed with the same fury she'd seen in his gaze years ago. She felt like that young lass who was being told what to do by everyone. The lass she was no longer. "I dinnae like his attitude toward our clan these days. It needs to change."

"You have not changed at all, have you, Broden? Did you ever consider that Royce is still upset that you rejected his suit, even after all these years? No matter. What does matter is that you can no longer tell me what to do. I was controlled by one cruel man, and I refuse to be controlled by any other. You are my younger brother, not my keeper."

"The hell I'm no' yer keeper! All of Scotland says the laird chooses who will marry his sisters. I am nae different. Ye know age doesnae have any measure in this issue, and ye'll no' marry Royce MacRob."

"I changed your raggies, Broden!" She stared up at her brother. His expression looked just like their father's when they'd been particularly naughty as children. His dark hair didn't appear to have any gray in it, yet his eyes bore a few cracks at the side, and she swore he had two wrinkles in his forehead. He carried the same responsibilities that their sire had. She'd been in awe of their father's strength and wisdom at one time, but he'd always looked old to her. Perhaps the strain of being laird through a feud had caused some of those changes.

"What do you have against Royce? You used to

play with him and his brothers all the time. Why do you hate him so?"

"'Tis none of yer concern."

"The hell it isn't. Your decision affects everything in my life. No more, Broden."

"Dinnae do it, Rhona! I'm giving ye fair warning no' to defy me. I'll no' have my sister running all over Scotland with an unmarried man. Ye'll totally destroy yer reputation."

She moved closer to her brother and whispered, "Broden, I do not care one wee bit about my reputation. I'll never marry again."

The look on his face told her their discussion was done. He would not budge on this matter.

Neither would she.

She marched over to the door with every intention of leaving without another word, but at the last minute, she spun around and bellowed at her obstinate brother, "I'll do what I want with my life. You will never tell me what to do again!"

Then she slammed the door behind her.

And lifted her face to the cool breeze and smiled.

CHAPTER SEVEN

THE DAY AFTER he'd ended things with Louisa, Royce sat on the dais in his great hall and wondered when he should approach Rhona about heading to Edinburgh. It would be best if they did not wait, because the deadline for the king to return was only a sennight away. If they left in the next day or two, they might catch him before he left Edinburgh. Or at least they might meet him along the road.

Mungo stood in front of him. "Aught special for the men, MacRob?"

"Nay, just practice their sword skills. This situation could turn dangerous quickly. I dinnae trust the MacAdders, even though Duncan is dead. His brother is ruthless and wants more land. And if Broden finds out Rhona and I plan to leave together, he could be stopping over for a visit, and I dinnae expect that to be a pleasant one either."

"Ye wish to go alone?"

"Nay, I will need three guards of yer choice. Should be enough. If Tor were here, I would take ye with us, Mungo, but ye must act as laird with both of us absent."

"I hope ye learn something about yer brother. I'll check with ye later."

As Mungo nodded and turned to go about his business, Royce noticed his friend had gained many gray hairs over the last few years. He had to wonder if the feud had anything to do with it. While his hair was generally unruly, it seemed even more so of late, his red hair peppered with gray standing out even more. He had to smile. His best friend had been loyal since birth and was thankfully married to a sweet woman who never complained about the demands on his time.

Hardly how Rhona would have been if they'd married.

His mother entered the hall, babbling on about her troubles in her usual way. He'd be lost without her and the skill with which she managed many of the clan's affairs. Still mistress of the keep, she oversaw the cooks and the housekeepers. He feared the day when it would prove too much for her, though she'd never admit it.

"Royce, we must make sure we build our stores up more. Signs point to a long winter, and we'll need the food. And Cook is carrying again, so I must find someone to take over for her when she has the bairn."

"Mama, please sit and relax."

She plopped into a chair, her smile there as always. "I'll handle it, Royce, though if ye'd find a wife, she could assist me. 'Twould be good if I had someone to pass all this on to, before I'm too decrepit to tell summer from winter. I must explain exactly how the caterpillars look when a long winter is due, and then explain about the butterflies and the hair on the nape of the cows. There is so much to pass along."

Royce scratched the back of his head as he continued to listen to his mother. He did love her dearly, but she was as relentless as his father had been. She was still an attractive woman and carried herself straight and tall. Though her hips had widened as she'd aged, her face held no wrinkles. His own held many more, he knew.

Losing Rhona and then his father had brought many of them.

"Royce, 'tis yer obligation to marry a lass and do it soon. Ye must! I know men can sire bairns for a long time, but ye shouldnae pick a lass too much younger than ye are or ye'll have trouble gettin' along."

"My thanks to ye, Mama, for yer worry, but I'll find the right lass soon." He used to argue with her that there was no one for him but Rhona, but he no longer bothered. It wasn't worth his time, and it only upset his mother more.

"If ye dinnae, ye could be next. Look at poor Tor, forced to marry a lass he cannae get along with. The king nearly chose ye. What think ye on that? Would ye like the king to choose for ye? I surely wouldnae. But 'tis yer duty to accept his decree, nae matter if ye like it or no'"

"Ye are correct. I'll search for one this day."

"And I'll go find Father Godfrey to let him know ye'll be marrying soon. But first I must speak with Cook about the meals for the morrow. About that lass, surely ye do agree with me? I'm sure that ye do." She sauntered away without waiting for his answer.

He breathed a quick sigh of relief once she was gone, then headed out the front door himself to find Mungo and the guards. He'd made his mind up, or rather Broden, the bastard, had made the decision easy for him. He would find Rhona and give her his answer about Edinburgh. Mungo had convinced him that it was best for them to speak with the king and promise to end this feud. In the process, if they could possibly find any sign of Ian and Marta or Tor and Ainsley, all would go much better. The king would leave them alone. He and Rhona could go back to living their lives apart.

He had to admit the prospect of traveling with her did hold a certain appeal. Their sex the other morn had been more than satisfactory, and he'd missed her hot temper. It could prove to be a pleasant journey.

Now that they suspected that Ian and Marta were in love instead of dead, the sense of urgency and each clan's desire for vengeance for some unknown injury had settled again. There was still the issue of the blood found near the river, but from the healer's tale, it seemed unlikely Ian had wielded the knife. If there was a third person involved, perhaps the couple had gone into hiding.

The healer had been vague about who had stabbed Marta, or the lass they all thought was Marta. All she'd been able to tell everyone for sure was that a couple had stopped for help, that the lass had survived a stabbing to her leg followed by a fever, and that they'd left because they were headed toward Berwick.

The couple had to be Ian and Marta. The healer's descriptions of them matched the missing pair, and their secrecy seemed in line with their disappearance. The two had refused to tell the healer who had injured the girl or who could be following them.

Who would they both fear? Was the stabbing intentional? If so, were they being followed? Was that why they left the healer and didn't return to Shaw or MacRob land? Were they running in fear for their lives?

It had to be someone they didn't know. He could think of no Shaw nor MacRob who would attack them, nor anyone else who lived among the nearby clans.

Either way, he wished to find them and bring them back. It was doubly important now—the command of the king to find them and end the feud had been the first push. But now, it seemed, finding them could be a matter of life and death. They had to find them before the villain did, whoever it may be.

As he neared the gates, a commotion started, and to his relief, it was one of joyful shouts and greetings. Mungo's loud voice carried to him. "Tor, ye daft bastard! Where the hell have ye been?"

He raced to the gates to see if he'd heard correctly.

There they were, the newly wedded couple,

and they both looked happy.

Happy?

They rode double on Tor's huge warhorse, a chestnut with a mane as dark as night, and he had one arm anchored securely around his bride's waist as if he couldn't bear to let her go.

"Brother, 'tis true? Yer wife rides in front of ye because ye wish it? Have ye nae more hate for each other?" He couldn't believe what his eyes told him, that Ainsley and Tor were now happily wed.

Tor dismounted, then reached for his wife, sliding her down his body and ending with a slow, hot kiss. The MacRob guards broke out in hoots and hollers. The pair broke apart, red tinging Ainsley's cheeks.

"Are ye in love, fool?" Royce asked as he clasped his brother's shoulder. He could barely be more surprised by the display he'd just seen.

"Aye, I'm in love and happy about it." He leaned over and kissed his wife hard on the lips.

Royce had no words. "What happened to ye?"

"Ainsley happened to me. Ye shouldnae be surprised. Ye felt the same about her sister at one time, nay?"

He couldn't argue with his brother, a bit of jealousy bubbling out of his gut. "I'm happy for ye, brother. Welcome to the clan, Ainsley."

Ainsley said, "We thank ye for the greetings, but we have news to share. Then I must find my sister. I know Rhona is worried about me."

"Come inside and refresh yerselves. Mama will wish to welcome ye and hear yer news."

The group moved inside, but their mother was nowhere to be found. Royce settled the couple with an ale and a platter of cheese and dark bread, then continued, "I hate to rush ye, but Rhona and I wish to go to Edinburgh and speak with Alexander. I was just on my way to her when ye arrived, but I'll wait to hear any news ye have first."

The door flew open and Mungo stood there, holding it open as Rhona hurried into the hall with a cry of joy. "Ainsley?"

The sisters both squealed, hugged, and giggled while Tor just shook his head. Royce couldn't help himself. He whispered to his brother, "Truly? Ye are in love?"

"Aye. I cannae say when or how, but we are verra happy together. 'Twas surely a trying journey in the beginning, but the trip home was quite enjoyable." Tor winked at his brother.

Royce broke into a loud guffaw, enough to stop the two sisters in the midst of their giggling and whispering. Then he said, "Come, Rhona. I was on my way to visit ye. I'm accepting yer offer to travel to Edinburgh, but first we must hear all these two have learned."

He stood up and pulled a chair out for Rhona, next to her sister.

"Take yer seat again, Ainsley, and Rhona will sit next to ye. I'm so pleased to see ye."

Ainsley sat, and Rhona nodded her thanks to Royce as he held her chair, then retrieved a glass of wine for her.

"You remembered?" she asked, blushing.

"Of course." He cleared his throat, afraid to look at Rhona for long and risk showing his feelings. The sight of his lass with a goblet of wine when everyone else raised tankards of ale was burned in his memory as permanently as the feel of her in his arms. She looked more beautiful than he'd ever seen her, her cheeks rosy from the joy of seeing her sister home. "Can ye believe yer sister claims to love my brother?"

Rhona looked up at him, and his heart did a flip just to have her smiling at him instead of cursing him. "Aye, I could not be happier for them."

While he knew she meant it, she wore an odd expression that he couldn't quite read.

He took in all that was Rhona for a long moment, and he had to force himself to draw his eyes from Rhona's lips and turn to his brother. "Tell us what ye know, please."

Tor leaned back in his chair, but not before taking his wife's hand in his. "The most shocking part is that we saw Marta and Ian near the marketplace."

"Truly?" Rhona asked. "Where? Which marketplace? Are they hale?"

"One question at a time, sister," Ainsley said. "I saw them in the marketplace in Berwick and pointed them out to Tor."

"Aye, it was them," Tor said. "I called out to the two when I saw them, and they both turned around, but then they disappeared in the crowd. We followed them but never caught up."

"Did they look hale?" Royce asked. "Was Marta limping at all?"

"They looked hale to both of us, but in a crowd, I couldnae see her leg or whether she favored it. Ian protected her well, standing behind her and keeping his arm around her."

Ainsley nodded. "I'm certain they are in love. They were so close, and Ian was quite protective of Marta."

"We have no idea why they were there, and we searched for a bit but decided we should bring the news back. We hope the knowledge that they are both alive and seem to be together willingly will stop the king from continuing his interference with our clans."

Royce's mother hurried through the door, lifting her skirts as she damn near ran toward them. "They have returned? Tor is . . . och, there ye be, my lad! Ye have come home and ye havenae killed yer bride yet, they tell me." The woman made her way over and hugged her son, dragging him out of the chair. Then she reached for Ainsley and pulled her up as well so she could give her a hug. "God bless ye, lassie, if ye have made my son happy. I'll forever be grateful that one"—she paused to glare at Royce—"of my sons is finally happily married."

Royce rolled his eyes behind his mother's back. "Mama, I'm pleased ye're happy, but would ye mind sitting for a wee bit? Tor and Ainsley were telling us what they've learned from their journey, and Rhona and I will be leaving for Edinburgh shortly. We must no' wait."

Royce gave Rhona a look to see if she still wanted to travel with him. She gave him a slight nod and a wee smile.

"Fine. Ye tell me all ye know, and then I'll tell ye that I cannae find Father Godfrey. I wish to tell him that Royce may be marrying soon, but he's gone."

Everyone spoke at once at that announcement, exclamations of surprise and protest filling the hall.

"Royce is gettin' married?" That came from Tor, a gleeful expression on his face.

"Who are you marrying?" Rhona's face was not gleeful.

Mungo, still by the door, shouted, "Cannae wait for the weddin'."

"I'm no' marrying anyone, Mama. Please dinnae say such things." Royce shoved out of his chair. "And where the hell is Father Godfrey?"

"I know where he is," Ainsley said.

"We saw him. 'Tis the other important thing we have to tell ye," Tor said. And again, everyone spoke at once, this time more questions than exclamations.

"Where did ye see him?"

"Berwick."

"He's no' on Shaw land?"

"What would he be doing in Berwick?"

"Father Godfrey never leaves unless the bishop summons him, and that would be to Edinburgh."

"He doesn't have a bishop in Berwick. It would have to be Edinburgh."

"I thought he was only to move between MacRob and Shaw property."

"Sometimes he goes to MacAdder's."

"Why would he go there?"

Finally Royce stood and said, "Quiet! Ye cannae all talk at once."

The melee quieted, so Royce sat down, nodding to Tor. "Tell us what ye learned."

His mother said, "Please tell me all ye've learned, Tor. I know I'm late, but ye can repeat some, briefly for me."

Tor told about seeing Ian and Marta in Berwick. "We dinnae know why they wouldnae stop to speak with us."

"They are afraid," his mother said, all eyes turning to her.

"Of course," Rhona said. "I believe you are correct, my lady."

His mother said, "My dear, ye nearly married my firstborn son. Please call me Helen. Go on, Tor."

"We saw Father Godfrey in Berwick also. Ainsley asked him why he was there, and he said he was ordered to come to Berwick by the bishop."

Their mother said, "'Tis most unusual. I dinnae recall him ever being called to see the bishop in Berwick. That would be Bishop Timlin. The man has lost his senses if he traveled to Berwick to see Bishop Timlin."

"I asked him why he was called to the bishop and why to Berwick," Ainsley said, "and he became flustered, made some excuse, and hurried off."

Tor glanced at his wife and asked, "Did ye no' think he was frazzled? Unkempt a bit?"

"Aye," Ainsley replied. "He looked as if he hadnae slept in a couple of days. His hair was askew and his chin stubbled. And then when we spoke with the bishop, he said he never summoned Father Godfrey."

His mother's eyes widened. "Father Godfrey? Och, nay. There must be something wrong. First the bishop tells a different story, and now ye tell me he's no' paying attention to his appearance? Nay, something is definitely wrong."

No one said anything, mulling over the information. Then his mother announced, "Royce, ye must go to Edinburgh. Ye must obtain an audience with the king and tell him all ye know. Find out why Father Godfrey went to see Bishop Timlin. Something fishy is happening. Something is awry. I can feel it in my bones. Ye must go right away."

Royce nodded. "I agree. Rhona, are ye willing to go with me?"

"Aye, but first I need to return to Shaw land and let Forsy know I'm leaving, say goodbye to my daughter, and speak with Broden."

"Now that Tor is home, Mungo, ye'll be joining us," he yelled over to his friend at the door.

Mungo nodded and said, "I'll be right back."

He knew where he was headed. He would let his wife know of his destination and his intended return. Mungo was another man in love with his wife, something one didn't see often.

His mind drifted back to Rhona and their plan, but he couldn't prevent another thought from popping into his mind. Royce thought of the expression he'd see on Broden's face when Rhona announced she was leaving with him. "I'd be pleased to escort ye, Rhona."

He kept the wide grin to himself.

CHAPTER EIGHT

R HONA RODE NEXT to Ainsley, now riding her own horse, while Royce rode abreast of Tor, the siblings chatting amongst themselves. Mungo led the group.

Rhona wasn't surprised to find Giric at the gate of Castle Shaw when they arrived. He opened the door and welcomed Ainsley home with a glad hail.

"I'll send a runner up to Broden," Giric said. "He'll be glad to see ye, Ainsley. Ye all can ride directly up, if that's yer destination." He signaled a lad, who took off for the hall, bearing the news of Ainsley's return.

"Tor and Ainsley will see my brother," Rhona said. "Do you know where I'll find Forsy and Annie? Royce and I are riding for Edinburgh, and I wish to bid them farewell before we go."

"They went inside for the midday meal. She's adjusting well, I believe. MacRob, who else is traveling with ye to Edinburgh? I can send guards along or I can join ye."

"Nay," Rhona said. "Please stay here, Giric. I'll feel better if you are watching over Annie and Forsy."

Giric nodded. "I'll speak with our laird. I'm sure he'll assign someone to go with ye."

Shouts of welcome greeted Ainsley as they walked through the courtyard, and Rhona nearly laughed over how possessive Tor was with his new wife, his arm never leaving her lower back.

They were acting exactly like she'd dreamed she and Royce would someday.

The someday that never came.

They stepped inside the hall as a group, not surprised to see Broden talking with a few guards, but he stopped as soon as his gaze fell on Ainsley. He headed directly toward them, ushering the guards out the door.

Rhona heard the delightful squeal of her daughter followed by her tiny feet on the stone floor as she headed toward her mother. Royce remained with her while Ainsley, Tor, and Broden gathered near the hearth, where they could speak privately.

"Mama! I have a new friend," Annie said, launching herself at her mother.

Rhona was so pleased to see the happiness in Annie's gaze. "Who is your new friend?"

"Her name is Eby. Her mother is the cook. May I play with her?"

"If her mother agrees, then you may. I'm happy you've found a new friend." She kissed her cheek and inhaled her daughter's unique sweetness. No matter what else had happened in her life, Annie was the gift from Heaven she was grateful for every day.

She caught Royce watching them, a wistful

look on his face. She understood. There had been a day she'd believed they'd share a bairn or five.

Forsy came after Annie, smiling as she nodded to Royce.

"Mama, who is your new friend?" Annie peered up at him, sudden recognition crossing her gaze. Rhona glanced back at him, wondering why she would recognize Royce.

"This is Laird Royce MacRob. You would call him *my lord*. He lives in the next castle and is a friend of mine. Say good day to him, sweetling."

Annie gazed up at him and said, "Good day, my lord." Then she returned her gaze to her mother. "I met him before, Mama."

Rhona had an odd feeling creep up her back. It continued all the way up her neck when she cast a glance back at Royce and his expression told her Annie's statement was indeed true.

"When did you meet?"

"When I filled the pitcher at the burn yestermorn. He helped me fill it so I would not fall in."

"My thanks to you for helping my daughter, Laird MacRob." She wanted an explanation for why he had been there, but she wouldn't bring it up in front of Forsy or her daughter. Her mother had taught her well to keep those questions private, or wagging tongues would change the question ten different ways.

Rhona knelt down in front of her daughter and pulled her attention back from Royce. "Mama is going away for a few days, Annie. Forsy will take good care of you while I'm gone. You may play with Eby when she's available, and Aunt Ainsley is back, so she will watch over you too."

Annie's eyes lit up as she noticed her aunt moving toward her. "Aunt Ainsley!"

She was about to run off, but Rhona held her back. "Mama will be back as soon as she can, but it will be at least a few days. I love you, sweet lassie."

"I love you too, Mama. I hope you come home quickly."

"As soon as I can." Rhona put a hand up to the corner of her eye to catch a tear before it fell. She'd never been away from her daughter for even a few hours, let alone a few days.

Annie patted her cheek. "Don't cry, Mama. I have many to watch over me now. I like the castle because it is so big and much warmer too. May I go see Aunt Ainsley now?"

"Of course you may." She stood, and her daughter took off in a rush toward her aunt.

Royce's voice came from behind her. "She's beautiful. She looks just like ye, Rhona."

"She does, doesn't she?" She couldn't stop the tears from rolling down her cheeks. "Mayhap I kept her hidden too long." They'd entered a new world, introducing Annie to the castle and her clanmates. Rhona couldn't help but notice that after Annie greeted Ainsley, she moved over to her uncle and climbed onto his lap. Broden kissed the top of her head and wrapped his arms around the wee lass as if he'd known her forever.

Had she harmed the only person in the world she'd wished to protect?

"Ye always protected Ainsley too. Ye had yer fists up anytime someone gave her an accidental shove." He gave a small imitation of her fighting stance when she was younger.

She glanced over her shoulder, wondering if she'd said the words so he could hear her or if he had read her mind.

Turning to face Royce, she said, "I did protect her whenever I could, and I'll do the same for my daughter."

"I would expect nae difference. Ye make a fine mother."

They said nothing for a moment, and in their stillness, a woman approached them, someone she didn't know. Obviously she knew Royce and very well. She leaned forward and spoke softly. "I couldnae help but overhear yer daughter. Royce was leaving my hut when he met yer daughter. He visited me often." Then she gave a saucy look to Royce and strolled out the door.

Royce's face turned furious, but he said nothing.

Rhona had to depend on her strength and self-control to ignore the woman the same way Royce had, but she managed. She strode over to her brother and said, "Royce and I will be going to Edinburgh. I trust you will watch over my daughter while I'm gone. Be on your best behavior, Annie." She blew her a kiss, gave Ainsley a hug, and whispered, "Please take good care of her."

When she turned away, the jealousy deep inside found its way to the surface. Who the hell was that woman, and what was her relationship with

Royce?

But Rhona had no business worrying about Royce's entanglements, since they had no relationship. Why shouldn't he be involved with a woman?

He might have mentioned the rude woman, though, or given her some thought before taking Rhona to bed the day before.

But he would have known what Rhona's reaction would be. Exactly how she felt now—ready to scratch the bitch's eyes out.

But she wouldn't. She had a daughter to think of now. And she and Royce had nothing.

She strode out of the great hall, never looking back.

~

Royce followed Rhona from the hall, not sparing a word or backward glance on Louisa.

It took longer than he liked to prepare for their journey—gathering the supplies they'd need on the road, loading the horses, and waiting to see if Broden would insist on sending guards with them, though he'd finally convinced him they didn't need any. Royce was eager to get away, and they needed to move quickly. Extra guards would only slow them down.

He'd promised Broden to bring Struan because of his archery skills along with Mungo and Tamhas, and that had satisfied him. He had a sudden need to finish this quickly and didn't truly care what Broden thought. This feud had gone on long enough, and if this journey could end it, he wanted to get on the road.

Twelve years.

Aye, he'd been angry with many people, but perhaps it was time to let it all go. After all, they could not go back and change anything.

Royce rode on one side of Rhona while Mungo was on the other. Now that Tor was home, Royce was glad to have his second along. They didn't expect to meet anybody this far into the Highlands, but the further south they moved, the more risk they'd take. They should arrive in Edinburgh the end of the next day, as long as there were no delays.

Reivers, thieves, wild boars. He hated wild boars. They could easily take you out with a tusk. The bold bastards would grunt at you and turn away, as if to dismiss you, then in the next moment, they'd be headed straight toward you.

And where there was one boar, there were likely more. The absolute worst was seeing a litter of wee ones. If they were small, the mother would be nearby, and she was always a mean bitch if she was protecting her young ones.

He hadn't seen any for a long time, so he hoped this trip would be free of the beasts.

Rhona said, "It has been a long time since I've ridden far. What do you worry most about? Reivers?"

There was no use in lying to her now that they were on their way. She needed to be aware of any possibilities. "Any thieves. 'Tis good weather, and they are most likely to be on cattle raids this time of year. We've worked hard on improving our sword skills, and I've practiced my archery too. Mungo is better with a sword, but one of the guards we brought along, Struan, is a better archer. He can nail a boar from a good distance away. We'll hope for a boring trip."

"I hope the weather stays fair. It's too warm for snow, but rain chills me to my bones. 'Tis what I missed the most in our small hut. A large hearth."

"Yer brother did no' provide ye a place with a good-sized hearth?"

"We only lived in a small cottage, but Giric found it for us, not Broden, and it was cold in the winter. You don't realize how the thick castle walls keep the wind out until you sleep in a thin-walled cottage. We had plenty of furs, but I was still cold, and so was Annie, especially when she was a babe."

"Ye were no' happy with MacAdder?"

She glanced over at him. "Nay, and I don't wish to talk about those days. And what of the woman who spoke to me before we left? Were you not happy with her?"

Royce stiffened. He'd known she would ask him eventually. He had nothing to hide. Rhona was married, and a man had his needs.

"Her name is Louisa. I did see her over the years. I never loved her, never felt more for her than gratitude. Consider her a friend."

Rhona arched a brow and gave him that challenging look he knew so well.

Royce added, "Aye, a close friend for a few years. The truth is that after I met ye at the hunting lodge, I told her I wouldnae be returning. She wasnae happy, though she had a man visiting at the time, so I hadnae been the only one to her."

"Were you aware of the other men in her life?"

"Nay." He said nothing more. There was no explanation for some things. He wasn't proud of many of his actions. Life had changed completely when he'd lost Rhona, but he wasn't ready to admit that to her yet.

"Does it bother you that she was seeing another man?"

"Nay. I did no' expect her loyalty. I promised her naught. I would never marry her, and she knew it." Hell, but did she have to probe so? He did not wish to discuss his private affairs with Rhona. His arrangement with Louisa was over, and that should be all that mattered. He wanted to just enjoy this time with Rhona. He'd missed her for so long that he cherished the ease of simply riding along beside her. He'd have paid dearly to do this with her once a year, once a moon. Any time.

"May I ask why you ended things with her?"

He considered his response for a moment. He would not be false with her. He didn't expect them to get back together at any time, but his answer might make her think he did. Still, he could not deny the truth. "After our time together the other day, I couldnae go back to her. My conscience wouldnae allow it."

"Because you were no longer faithful to her?"

How could she ask him such a question? Had she no idea of her value? What she meant to him? What she had meant so long ago? "Nay, because

I would feel unfaithful to ye, Rhona. How can ye no' see that?"

"Because I didn't promise you anything. It was probably the last time we'll be together, so I don't know why you would have interpreted it that way. We made no commitment to each other."

He cleared his throat and stared up at the sky. "I know all of that. It just felt wrong. I will never see Louisa again and may never speak to her except to tell her to keep her thoughts to herself. She had no right to approach ye at all. 'Twas jealousy that made her speak to ye. I know it, and I think ye do too."

"I suspect you're right." She stared straight ahead, sitting her horse as if she were a regal queen. "If it means anything, I feel the same way."

That did mean something. After all these years, he knew she hadn't married the man of her own free will. Truthfully, he'd always known. He had to stop blaming her, and now that she was out of hiding, seeing her brought back many old feelings. Those few words gave him a wee bit of hope. He'd cling to it.

CHAPTER NINE

RHONA SETTLED ON the ground, one fur underneath her and another over her. She'd worn a pair of trews under her gown for extra warmth and comfort. Her mother would tell her ladies didn't wear trews, but she wasn't sleeping on the ground with only wool hose on.

Royce had offered her another plaid, and his own body heat along with it, but the furs were enough.

"Last time I'll offer to lie next to ye to keep ye warm, lass. I know how cold the ground is, and I'm no' convinced ye do."

"Royce, I appreciate your offer, but you'd be surprised what I've survived over the last twelve years. I'll be fine. As long as it does not rain, I'll be warm enough." If Duncan MacAdder's fists couldn't destroy her, a wee bit of cold wouldn't hurt her.

"I think ye are safe, then." He turned his attention to Mungo. "I'll take first watch tonight."

As Royce and Mungo divided up the rest of the night's watches between Mungo, Struan, and the other guard, Tamhas, Rhona had the feeling that all would be fine this night, so she curled up as close to the smoldering coals of the fire as possible and closed her eyes.

She woke up to darkness and an eerie feeling that she was being watched. Then the cold hit, cutting through grogginess. Tremors shook her entire body.

A voice reached her from behind, "Do no' move, lass."

Any Highlander knew to mind such a command, in such a low, urgent tone, so the only thing she moved was her eyes, praying they would adjust to the dark of the night quickly enough to determine what exactly was happening. A moment later, she saw motion across the remains of their fire.

A mere horse's length away stood three boar piglets, their mother behind them. The grunting sow warned all who heard to stay away from her bairns. Wild boars could be quite mean, but none worse than a mother protecting her young.

"Royce?"

The warmth of his breath crossed her ear, and she nearly sighed with a gratitude he wouldn't understand. "I'm here. I'd move in front of ye, but 'twould be too much movement, and she'd see it as a threat." His hand moved in front of her, a long dagger gripped tightly in the palm of his hand. "I'll protect ye. Dinnae worry."

"Damn easy for you to say."

He let out a small chuckle, the kind she'd heard so many times before he'd go into hysterics, but he controlled himself. He didn't move but said, "Struan, where the hell are ye? Ye need to take her out. She's ready to attack, just sniffing out who she wishes to charge first."

"Well, she knows better than tasting yer sorry arse," Mungo drawled, his voice coming from her right.

"Looks like an entire pig for each of us," Tamhas said, coming from her left.

A few moments later, all hell broke loose. An arrow sluiced through the air, catching the mother in her flank. The beast squealed and charged straight ahead, straight at Rhona. Two more arrows hit the piglets, while the remaining piglet squealed and ran next to its mother.

Rhona jumped up and nearly fell when Royce shoved her behind him. He flung his dagger at the squealing mother while Tamhas took position, bracing his spear against the ground right in her path. The mad beast ran herself onto the spear's head with more strength than any man could have put behind a thrust. She fought no more.

Blood was everywhere while the four men cleaned and dressed the animals.

Rhona grabbed a nearby tree, unsure whether she was about to heave her insides out all over the forest or pass out from the fear of nearly being a snack for a big boar and its piglets. She'd been hiding for so long that she hadn't faced this kind of fear for five years, but it quickly brought back images of fists flying at her along with degrading insults.

She should have been able to put all that behind her at this point.

Royce reached for her just as her knees

crumpled. She would surely land on the ground and knock herself in the head, but for his strength, she didn't.

His warm arms wrapped around her, and he grabbed a plaid from the ground to cover her, holding her tight. "Hush, ye'll be fine. The beast willnae bother ye again, lass."

"Royce," she said, gripping his tunic for dear life. "I don't know how to tell you this, but I'm no longer a lass."

"Ye'll always be my lass." His whispered words warmed her, and she lost all control. That rigid stance she held for so long gave way, lost to the comfort of this dear man who she loved with all her heart, who would protect her instead of hurt her. Love her instead of hate her.

A man she knew, without a doubt, would never raise a hand to her.

She sobbed against him for a few moments, even noticed Struan came toward them to show off one of the dead animals. Mungo's voice stopped the young guard in his tracks, and he dropped his gaze and turned around.

"Rhona, ye are breathin' too fast. Take some nice slow, deep breaths," he said, his strong arm still supporting her.

She did what he suggested, and it helped. She should have realized. She'd told Annie the same thing when she was upset about something. "I'll be fine, Royce. You can let me go."

"Nay, I willnae. I know ye. Ye'll no' be able to sleep at all. So ye'll lie in my arms and they'll be nae arguing."

"All right. I'm tired. May I please close my eyes?"

He fetched her furs, then settled her on the ground under an oak tree with thick leaves to protect them should it rain. Then he nestled behind her, her arse against his groin, and yet she didn't care how close they were. "I promise to be proper with ye, Rhona. Ye sleep, and I'll protect ye."

She nearly fell asleep, but then thought better of it. She had something to do. "Royce, my thanks to you for protecting me. You always did."

"And I always will."

~

Royce awakened to a scream.

Rhona flailed, hitting at some unknown object, but her eyes were still closed.

"Royce?" Mungo shouted. "Do ye need help?"

"Nay, she's dreaming. I'll awaken her and settle her."

The more he talked, the harder her arms moved.

"Rhona," he said, taking a hold of her arms.

"Let me go, you mean bastard."

Ah, she was attempting to fight off her husband, he suspected. "Wake up, my lass. 'Tis Royce, no' Duncan. Duncan is dead."

"Royce? Royce, please help me. He will not leave me be." Her voice changed, a tone that spoke of fear, not the strength and stubbornness he'd seen in her so often. She sounded like a woman whose every movement, word, and thought was controlled. It nearly made him weep to hear it.

"I'm here, Rhona. Duncan is no'. We're in the forest, heading to Edinburgh to see the king. Annie is with yer sister, Ainsley."

She rolled over to face him and opened her eyes. "Annie? She is hale?"

"Annie is fine. She is with Giric, Forsy, Broden, Catlin, Ainsley and Tor. No' a one of them would allow any harm to come to her." He traced his finger down her jawline, swiping away a tear that had trailed down her cheek.

"I'm sorry I woke you. I was dreaming. Duncan was . . . go back to sleep. I'll be fine."

He doubted she would be. Perhaps if she spoke of the pain in her marriage, she could help put it behind her. "Ye were dreaming of the time after Annie was born?"

"Nay," she said, a wee bit too quickly. "It was one of the usual times."

Royce hated to ask the question. He wouldn't like the answer, and the man was already dead, so he could not make him pay for his crimes. But he had to know.

"Usual times? He beat ye often?"

After snuggling back up against him, she sighed and whispered, "He liked to tie me to the bed. I was not allowed to move while he took what he wanted. I hated every moment I spent with the man, but being tied up was so much worse. Humiliating and degrading. He did it so I couldn't hit him, of that I'm sure. I did connect with his face once, the first time. I was so helpless, so . . ."

"He'll never hurt ye again, but ye know that.

How can I help ye?"

"You already helped me to get through each time with him. I would always close my eyes and think of you. I would relive one of our times together. It was the only way I could hold on to my mind, to keep any will at all."

"I knew he beat ye because Annie wasnae a lad, but did he beat ye on a regular basis?"

"Nay. A few times, especially in the beginning, because I talked back to him. And he struck my knuckles whenever I spoke with a burr. That's why I don't speak with a Scots' tongue anymore." She brought her hand up to show him the two fingers that were disfigured and scarred. "It was a thin stick with three finely chiseled points, each one to hit one of my fingers. I learned to speak like an English woman very quickly."

He took her hand and kissed each of her scarred knuckles. "Had I known, I would have beaten the devil sooner."

She turned her head to look at him and asked, "You beat him? When?"

"After ye gave birth, word traveled among the guards. We heard he beat ye in the hall for all to watch. I could no' allow that to go unpunished. I waited until one night he was on the way to visit one of his mistresses. He was alone. I waited until he was far enough away so no one would hear. I came out from the trees and dragged him off his horse. Then I beat him until he couldnae speak. I told him if he ever touched ye again, I'd return, and the next time would be worse."

Rhona cupped his cheek. "I had no idea you

did that for me. I wish I had seen him. That would have pleased me very much." She smiled a wee bit, and he kissed her palm. "I hit him that day after Annie's birth. That was why he had his brother and his second hold me."

"Proud of ye, lass. He needed two men to hold ye down. I'd be bragging about that." She probably couldn't see him in the dark, but he grinned. "And I'm glad to see he couldnae break yer spirit. Ye are a strong woman, Rhona."

"He nearly did so many times. It was so difficult. I never knew what would set his temper off. His yelling was bad enough. I appreciate you giving him his just due for me, Royce."

"I was so angry I had to retaliate somehow. I dinnae like big men who beat on people smaller than they are."

"Oh, Royce. How I wish things could have been different. We were so good together."

"We still could be, Rhona, if ye'd give us a try." He couldn't believe the words that just came out of his mouth. Hadn't he refused her offer only days ago?

He knew why his mind had changed. She was in his arms, and he wanted to protect her forever. He also had enough pride that knowing she hated her husband from the very beginning eased his jealousy, his sense of betrayal. Mungo had been right. He'd probably never get over Rhona. She was in his blood. Now all he had to do was convince her that they still belonged together, even after twelve years.

She rolled onto her side away from him and

said, "It is too late."

"Why? We could marry and put an end to all this. Is that no' what ye wanted?"

"Aye, but . . ." Her eyes closed, and in the next moment, her breathing had deepened into that of sleep.

He was not about to let this go, but he would allow her to rest.

CHAPTER TEN

RHONA AWAKENED THE next morn, surprised to find herself tucked against Royce, a light snore coming from him. She smiled, cherishing this cozy moment with him. They would have indeed been wonderful together.

His breathing changed, and he nuzzled her neck. "Good morn to ye, my wee beauty."

"Good morn." She lifted her head to scan the area. "There are no more wild pigs about, are there?" She noticed Mungo returning through the bushes, a smile on his face, and the other men were up and about.

"Nay, no more beasts to frighten ye."

She pushed away from Royce and whispered, "I must go visit the bushes myself, but I . . ."

"Dinnae worry. I'll check and find ye a safe area." He jumped to his feet and held his hand down to her to help her stand, then held his hand up. "I'll be right back."

While she waited, she folded her furs and placed them back on her horse. Around her, the others were doing the same with their own furs and plaids.

"Pork for breakfast, for sure," Mungo said with

a grin.

Struan crouched by the fire, which snapped and crackled in the morning stillness. "I've got some already cooking. Cannae wait for a nice big slice of roasted pig."

Rhona's belly gave a wee twist of hunger—the scent of the roasting meat made her mouth water—but it wouldn't be ready to eat for a time yet. Royce returned and guided her to a well-hidden area near a burn not far from their camp. She hurried to take care of her needs, then sat on a rock where she could reach the fresh water and splash her face and hands liberally. The frigid water made her gasp but refreshed her. Her thoughts went to her daughter, wondering how she fared, having her mother away for so long. She thought of her dear Annie nearly every moment of the day, and she had to remind herself constantly to focus on her purpose.

She lingered by the stream, thinking on all that had taken place. The wild sow's attack, Royce coming to protect her, much as he always had. She wasn't entirely sure why she had sobbed so hard after all was done and quiet again. She hadn't wept like that since the early days of her marriage, before she'd toughened.

And Royce had held her through the entire thing.

Then he'd held her close, tucking her tight, behaving like the gentleman he was, while she spoke of all that had happened to her.

Well, not all, but enough for him to understand what her life had been like.

And why she hated her brother. She'd made peace for the good of her daughter and to help end the feud, but she hadn't forgiven him.

She had no worries about Louisa, not after his care this past night. Royce had been alone for twelve years. Someday she would ask him why he'd never married.

She would have been destroyed if he'd ever chosen another.

Running her fingers through her hair and twisting it back into a neat plait, she had a vague recollection of a nightmare and Royce awakening her, but she wasn't quite sure. Hadn't she dreamt of Duncan and that was when she decided to tell Royce how her life had been?

Had he told her he had followed Duncan and beaten him after he'd heard of what Duncan had done to her?

She scratched her head, her mind fuzzy from lack of sleep and fear. In fact, they'd had quite a few close moments . . . but she couldn't quite pull them all back.

A sound came from the clearing, Royce's voice and Mungo's calling out to someone. She hurried back, wondering who could be approaching.

She said a quick prayer that it would not be reivers or thieves.

To her surprise, it was the healer Forsy had brought to their cottage a couple of times. She was with a man who looked to be her husband. She stepped into the clearing, and Royce reached for her, took her by the hand and tugged her up next to him.

"Where are ye headed, Odart?" Royce asked.

"Ahhh, we are going to another clan. Heard they need healers and we cover a few clans, no' just the Shaws and MacRobs," the man said, giving his wife an odd look. Rhona suspected that maybe the healer would have a different tale. And indeed, Eufemie proved Rhona's suspicions right in the next moment.

"'Tis no' all," the older woman said through a clenched jaw. "We are thinking of going to Edinburgh."

"Why?" Mungo asked, his eyes narrowing while he assessed the two.

"Ye need no' tell them all, Eufemie." Odart glanced at his wife and nodded. "We'll be on our way. Fare thee well."

"Odart, no reason to lie. We are going to report our suspicions about the priest and the young couple. When we heard from Mistress MacRob that Father Godfrey was missing, I recalled that the lass called out, 'Father, nay,' when she was in the fever. We thought she meant her sire, but mayhap she meant the priest. 'Tis nagging at me. Odart's hoping to pick up an odd job or two along the way for some coin also. First, we must heal. But I feel better telling ye about our suspicions." She glared at her husband and brushed the stray hairs back from her face, her gaze falling on the roasting pork. "Laird MacRob, we'd feel better if ye did something with this information, since ye are a laird and can take action to save the lad and lass. We'll be on our way to find our work now, and no' go to Edinburgh, since 'tis out of our way."

"My thanks to ye, Eufemie. We'll consider it." Royce nodded to her and they headed back to their horses.

"Wait," Royce hollered as they moved along.

"We didnae do aught wrong," Odart declared. "We were just trying to help at the wedding."

A look passed from Royce to Mungo and back again, so she knew they were suspicious of something too. The older couple shifted and edged away, Eufemie tipping her head to tell her husband they needed to go. "We arenae going to beg, Odart."

Royce said, "We've been roasting some pork after killing a boar last eve. We have much to share. Take some with ye."

The relief on Odart's face was obvious. He smiled and said, "We'd be much obliged. We havenae eaten much more than an oatcake, and the aroma was what brought us this way."

Struan sliced and wrapped some of the cooked pork and handed it to Odart.

"Thank ye all, and Godspeed to ye." Odart added, "Many thanks for the meat."

And they were gone.

"What was that about?" Rhona asked, forgetting all her thoughts about the middle of the night. "I was not at the wedding. What exactly did they say then?"

Royce explained, "Those are the two who helped us all believe the pair must have been Marta and Ian. The lass's knife wound would account for the blood found by the river. They came to Catlin's wedding and told some of the tale there. Ye heard the story, aye?"

"Forsy did tell me that much. Why did they look and act so guilty just now? Or did I imagine that?"

"Nay, they definitely looked guilty," Struan said. "They couldnae wait to get away from us."

"Except Odart wanted the meat."

Rhona added, "And he lied. His wife did not like that. I think that's why she was upset. I believe what she said." Then she grinned. "And a man must have his meat. He was probably a long way from here and dragged her this way."

The men all laughed about that, but Rhona couldn't get the story out of her mind.

"What's wrong?" Royce asked.

"Something about that story. Could it be that Marta was referring to her own father instead of the priest? I wish you knew Marta's father better. Would he go after them? Would he have hurt Ian or Marta?"

Struan said, "Though he is a carpenter, he went on many of the patrols, but we found naught. He was upset each time. He could have gone after them, but I doubt he would have hurt his own daughter."

"Tell me again how the story went?" Rhona asked Royce.

Royce said, "The couple was verra mysterious about the injury, and then she had the fever for a few days. As soon as she healed from that, the two insisted they had to leave. They went south, and until Tor and Ainsley returned, that was all we knew."

Mungo added, "Marta does have an aunt in Berwick, so we thought she could be headed that way."

"Aye, 'tis where Tor and Ainsley saw the couple." Royce scratched his head. "The healers dinnae look like the traveling kind. Do ye think they know more than they are telling?"

"Aye," Rhona said. "They know more than they are saying. I'm sure of that much. If Marta and Ian never show up, I would definitely go to that couple for more information."

They rode through the day in peace, and the sun was halfway down the sky when they saw Edinburgh in the distance. Royce had to admit his bones were getting old. He wanted a real bed, and if he had his way, Rhona would be next to him.

She'd been quiet since they'd met the healers, though. She hadn't mentioned any of their discussion from the night before, but he guessed that was because of the audience they had.

He'd wait and speak with her more when they were alone.

As they reached the outskirts of the burgh of Edinburgh, the castle looming over them from the top of the hill, Mungo asked, "Do ye plan to go straight to the castle? See if the king is in residence?"

"Aye, and if he is, I plan to stay there. Rhona

can spend the night in the castle also. Ye three can stay at an inn, and I'll meet with ye in the morning."

They found a comfortable lodging for the guards, then split up, Royce and Rhona riding up the steep road to the castle itself.

Rhona glanced at Royce. "Do you think we'll be allowed to stay at the castle tonight? I surely would love a warm, soft bed."

"I see no reason no'. The king usually provides lodging for any lairds and their wives."

"Except I'm not your wife, and we are currently not in his favor."

He reached over and ran his finger up her neck to her chin. "Is that no' why we're here? To convince him to favor us again? Before we enter, we need to be sure we know exactly what we are offering. At one time ye wished to offer marriage. Last eve ye were no' so sure." He could tell by the look on her face that she was uncertain. "Tell me yer thoughts, Rhona. I cannae decipher where yer mind is at. In our lodge, ye suggested we marry to gain the king's favor. I suggested it last night and ye just said nay before ye fell asleep. Why did ye have a change of heart?"

They arrived before Rhona could answer. At the gate, he was questioned as to their purpose. "Laird of Clan MacRob and eldest sister of the Shaw laird here to see King Alexander. We respectfully request an audience with our king and two chambers for the night."

They were allowed through the thick outer wall and into the large castle courtyard, guards everywhere they looked. A stableman stepped forward as if he'd been waiting for them. "We'll care for yer horses. Step inside to speak with His Majesty's steward."

Royce put his hand at the small of Rhona's back, which gave him more pleasure than he would have guessed. He had to admit having Rhona near was the most pleasure he'd had in he didn't know how long.

That was a falsehood—he *did* know how long. Twelve years. And that brought home a truth he couldn't deny—he was still in love with Rhona. Would always love her.

But something was still wrong with Rhona.

"Lass, before we step inside, ye should decide if ye'll marry me or no'. Is this what we're offering King Alexander in return for an end to the forced marriages? 'Tis what ye wished for, is it no'?"

Rhona turned to him, her eyes shining with tears. "I'm not sure, but I must ask you. If we marry, would you keep a mistress? Would you continue to see Louisa or some other?"

She blinked, and her tears were gone as she locked her gaze on his.

Royce tugged her aside to an empty spot in the courtyard. "How can ye ask me such a thing?"

"Because many men do keep mistresses, and you've been with Louisa for a long time. The time you spent with her before is none of my concern. But it is my concern if there is a mistress that you cannot break away from. Will there be another woman somewhere along the way? Will you tire of this old woman? I'm no longer young.

You are the laird. I know the lasses will smile sweetly at you." Then her arms flew in the air in frustration. "I don't know what I'm talking about. It's just . . ."

He had a sudden idea where her questions were coming from. "How many mistresses did MacAdder have? Or perhaps I should ask how soon he started spending time with a mistress?"

She rolled her eyes and stared off to the side. "The day after our wedding. And I was told he had more than five he visited regularly."

"That many? Ah, lass. Ye have good reason to wonder, then."

She nodded, still not looking at him. He set his finger under her chin and pulled her gaze back to his. "He was a fool. And I am no'. Please remember that."

He wished to rail at her for being so foolish, but he held his tongue. Ah, he loved this stubborn, outspoken lass. Her jealousy told him that she still loved him. A new hope that they could make this work blossomed inside him. That they could marry and be happy.

"Rhona, ye are the only one I've ever loved. I have nae feelings for Louisa nor any other lass. I am no' interested in a young lassie who spends her time acting like a fool. If ye are back in my life, I want nae others. 'Tis ye and only ye."

"Duncan had several." Again she stared at the ground.

"Dinnae consider me the same as yer husband. We are naught alike. I see ye must know the entire truth. I went to Louisa to ask her to spy on ye."

"Spy on me?" Her voice had a tinge of anger.

"Aye. I couldnae handle no' knowing if ye were safe and hale. Once I learned ye were on Shaw land, I had to know if ye remained there. I didnae know if MacAdder would come for ye and force ye back to his castle. I wasnae on speaking terms with yer brother or any other Shaw, so 'twas the only way I could learn of yer whereabouts. I didnae know if Broden had threatened MacAdder or if he was watching over ye. So I found someone who would watch what happened, who could ask questions in the great hall, and keep me abreast of yer whereabouts. 'Tis the only reason I approached her. Mungo gave me her name, which he learned from a member of Clan Shaw he trusted."

"So she wasnae yer mistress? I dinnae understand."

"'Twas what she wanted in return. I agreed. I had nae one and my manhood had a way of betraying me after a while." He gave her a sheepish look, but she continued to stare. Then she dropped her gaze. He gave her the time to think, only offering one more comment. "Ye are the only one for me, Rhona. Always and forever. After twelve cold winters, nae one else tempts me. I love ye."

"I did not expect you to be a saint, Royce. I accept your explanation, but I still need a bit of time to think. You had someone spy on me for a very long time. Does that mean you'll have someone spy on me if we are married?"

"Nay. If we marry, we'll be together, and 'twill

be easier to protect ye, as I must do. I've needed to protect ye from the day I took yer maidenhead. I couldnae live worrying about ye every day, where ye were, whether yer husband had come for ye. I had to know. I will always protect ye, but I would no' hire a spy for my wife."

He could almost read what crossed her mind. Being spied upon made her uncomfortable, unclean. But should she not be happy that he worried about her enough to go to the trouble to find someone to spy on her?

"So much has happened in such a short period of time."

"I understand. 'Tis late in the day. Let's go speak with the steward and see if we can gain an audience. Probably willnae be until the morrow, but if we dinnae ask soon, there may no' be chambers for us."

"I'd prefer not to have to go back down to the burgh and climb this hill again in the morn. I do not have an answer for you about marriage, Royce. I need more time to think." Rhona smiled gently and squeezed his hand.

They stepped into the castle, and a guard led them down several passageways until they finally stopped at a small alcove, where a man sat behind a table and studied a number of documents in front of him.

Royce stepped up to the table and waited for the man to acknowledge them. He kept his hand at the small of Rhona's back, wanting to keep her close, but keenly aware of the propriety required while in the king's residence.

The small man didn't notice them at first, and when he finally looked up, his eyes widened, and he bolted out of his seat. "Aye, my lord?"

"I am Laird Royce MacRob and this is . . ."

"I know who ye are." He fiddled with his papers, tugged on the neck of his collar, then sat down again. "And ye are Lady MacAdder," he said, nodding to Rhona as he used her legal title. Royce felt her shiver at the name. "Good eve, my lady."

Royce said, "We've come to request an audience with King Alexander and to beg hospitality for the night, chambers next to each other, if possible."

"We only have one chamber left," the steward said, scanning his papers.

"Fine. She will sleep inside, and I'll sleep outside her door."

"We dinnae . . ."

"Ye dare to question that I protect Laird Shaw's sister?"

"Nay, nay," he stammered, dropping a piece of parchment. "That will be acceptable. I will inquire if our king will make himself available." He hurried away, tripping on a hump in the carpet along the way.

"We'll probably no' be able to see Alexander until the morrow, but 'tis soon enough."

"Aye. I'm quite tired," Rhona said.

The assistant stepped inside a door down the passageway and wasn't there for more than a few moments before he returned. "King Alexander will see you now, my lord. This way, Laird MacRob, Lady MacAdder."

"My thanks to ye," he said, ushering Rhona in front of him as a footman held the door. Two guards stood to either side of the opening, though neither spoke.

"Get in here, MacRob. We must speak."

Royce looked at Rhona, surprised at the tone of the king's voice.

"Hurry yourselves over here and everyone else out."

CHAPTER ELEVEN

RHONA LEANED AGAINST Royce, afraid the trembling in her legs would cause her to crumple to the ground. She knew, without a doubt, that Royce would catch her. This chamber was smaller than she would guess the main hall would be, but it was cozier, the large hearth warming the chamber. The king sat at a small table near the hearth, in the glow of the fire. A few trestle tables off to the side, empty now, stood ready for members of the court or other attendants.

The others in the hall scrambled to leave, casting a glance at the newcomers. Most were men, but there was one beautiful woman who made a point of pausing across from Royce, doing her best to draw his gaze. He seemed not to notice her. He was more interested in looking around the small hall, at the weaponry displayed on the walls, and the ornate woodworking on the furniture.

A booming voice called out to him. "I tire of this feud of your clan's, MacRob." When he noticed Rhona, he dropped his voice and moderated his tone. "And yours also, my lady." He beckoned them both forward. He sat on a dais with a platter of cheese and fruit on the table before him. "Sit so we may discuss this. I do not look forward to traveling to Shaw land again to force another marriage. Have you found the young couple or not?"

Royce helped Rhona into her chair, then took the seat next to her. "We have no' located the couple."

"Then why are you here?" he asked, his irritation no less obvious despite his low tone.

Rhona spoke up. "Because we did as you bid our clans to do—searched for them. We know they are alive. They were seen by a healer, and also by my sister and Laird MacRob's brother in Berwick. Marta has an aunt living in Berwick, and it's likely they're with her. But they were seen together. Both are very much alive."

This would not be enough for their king. She knew it as soon as the words left her lips.

There was only one way to be certain this man didn't force any more marriages on their clan, and it was now in her hands. She glanced over at Royce, and he gave her a small smile of encouragement.

A short time ago in a hunting lodge, she had begged him to marry her, and he had refused.

Now he'd asked her, and she had refused.

What had she been thinking? This was Royce MacRob. The man she'd loved with all her heart—the man she *still* loved so very much—the man she'd kept in her dreams, who'd helped her through the worst situations imaginable, and the man she deserved. There was no more believing all the awful things Duncan MacAdder had told her, that she was lacking in so many ways.

But Royce never thought her lacking. He never had and he didn't now. Perhaps it was time to accept his suit, marry him, and live the life she'd longed for. Let her dearest daughter see how wonderful life could be, teach her what a blessing it was to have strong men in her life.

She missed Annie with every breath she took, but the lass had been cheated of belonging to a clan, of being surrounded by others who loved her. Of learning what true love was.

The king paused, his gaze going from Rhona to Royce. "You are the couple who was the cause of the feud long ago, are you not? Rhona Shaw MacAdder, Broden's eldest sister, and Royce MacRob, laird of the mighty Clan MacRob. What have you to offer me? Until the couple tells their tale to one laird or the other and the feud is ended, I'll continue to impose my will upon you both. I tire of your animosity. It must end."

Royce started to speak, but she squeezed his hand and he stopped. She spoke, a bit of a tremor in her voice. "We are willing to offer marriage but would ask that Father Godfrey marry us. If he is available."

The king looked from her to Royce, then aimed his question at him. "You and Rhona are willing to marry now? Do you agree, Laird MacRob?"

He nodded, squeezing her hand, the smile on his face telling her how pleased he was with her suggestion. "I am, if she is. We've wanted this for a long time, Yer Majesty." Royce looked at her and asked, "Ye're sure about this?"

"Aye," she said, looking back at him. His face lit up from hearing her single word. "This is exactly what I want." She still loved him as much as she had in the days when they'd been foolish young lovers. She couldn't stop the tears from misting her gaze.

"Are you crying because he's forcing your hand in this marriage?"

She shook her head with equal parts irritation and certainty. "Nay, my brother forced my marriage, not this man. Never this man. I trust Royce above all others."

King Alexander leaned forward and arched a brow at her.

"Well, of course I trust my king over all, but Royce would be next." She blushed, catching Royce's smirk out of the corner of her eye.

The king resettled in his chair. "I had my secretary do some research in the archives, and his findings reminded me of the original feud that erupted because of you. It seems that if you had married twelve years ago, there would not have been a feud. So why did you not? I'm constantly bombarded with chaos because of you—letters from lairds, reports from my sheriffs. Even my bards sing about you two. Give me a good reason I should be merciful in my judgment."

A sudden fury rose up in Rhona. How dare he say the feud was *their* fault? "May I speak honestly, Your Majesty?"

"Please do, my lady."

She cleared her throat. "If not for your complicity, we could have married. I would never have married Duncan MacAdder without being forced. I loved Royce, and we planned to marry until MacAdder produced the agreement between my sire and him, which you signed."

"What agreement? I never signed any document of MacAdder's that I recall."

Royce, his cheeks turning a bit red, asked, "Ye did no' sign a betrothal agreement, granting Duncan MacAdder the right to take one of the Shaw laird's daughters as his wife?"

The king snorted, quite indelicately. "Nay. I would never have signed such a ridiculous statement. Not for MacAdder. I knew your father well, Rhona. He would have been pleased to see you married to Laird MacRob and deeply sorrowed to see you held by that other."

Royce and Rhona both began to laugh, the kind of desperate laugh that comes when the only other option is to wail. Indeed, Rhona's laughter soon turned to tears. Her marriage, the years of abuse, the cruelty, the intimidation had all come out of a deception by Duncan? The thought was preposterous. All these years she could have been happily married to Royce, given him bairns, lived in a castle instead of a prison and then a hut. But Duncan had forged some document as proof and her brother had believed it. It couldn't be.

Twelve years of her life lost to a lie. It was too difficult to believe. She wished to deny it, reject what she'd learned. The thought was too painful. Her tears became wrenching sobs.

"Enough. I'll have no tears in the king's chambers. Do you need to leave to compose yourself, my lady?"

"Nay." Her voice came out in a whisper, and she dried her tears with a linen square. "I cannot believe that Duncan forged your signature, Your Majesty. It is difficult for me to absorb that all that happened over twelve years' time was for naught." The somersaults in her belly would not stop.

"Rest assured, he would be arrested immediately and shown no mercy if he were still alive. Forging the king's signature would bring a charge of treason. Such a document should have raised questions for your brother."

Rhona thought of Broden, how young he'd been then, not even twenty. "My brother had just taken over the lairdship. We both still grieved for our sire. He was so young."

"And foolish," King Alexander said. "Not uncommon for new lairds. I'm sure MacAdder knew he could take advantage of his grief and his innocence and timed his move for that purpose. MacAdder was wily and conniving. No doubt about that. I will have to keep an eye on his brother and ensure that your daughter is not denied her rightful place as MacAdder's heir."

The three quieted, Rhona frozen by the thought that one day Annie might be the lady of MacAdder Castle. Royce squeezed her hand, as if he could sense her turmoil.

"Yer Majesty," Royce said at last, "I'd be pleased to marry Rhona right now even though we cannae have Father Godfrey marry us."

"You could have Father Godfrey marry you. Why not just go home and have him marry you?"

"It would please my mother. She adores him," Royce added. "But he told my brother several days ago that he had been summoned to Berwick, so 'tis where he is at present. He's no' on MacRob land or my mother would have found him."

The king gave an indelicate snort. "He's not in Berwick to my knowledge. Father Godfrey has no reason to be there. His bishop is here in Edinburgh, not Berwick. There is no reason for him to be in Berwick."

Rhona and Royce exchanged a glance, then turned back to the king. Rhona said, "Your Majesty, my sister saw him in Berwick the same day she and Tor saw Ian and Marta there. They spoke, and Father Godfrey said he was summoned by the bishop."

"Then something is awry. Berwick is hardly on the way from the Highlands to Edinburgh. I've heard of no summoning, and I was under the impression that he'd been given express orders to stay in your parish. I'll talk to the bishop here as he is the one who would have given him any orders. If he knows of no reason for Father Godfrey to be in Berwick, he may take further action."

Rhona had no idea what that meant, but she didn't ask. Church law was beyond her knowledge.

"Back to the matter at hand," the king continued. "You say the young couple has been seen, but is there an explanation for the blood that was found?"

Royce nodded. "The healer who came to my

sister's wedding said she stitched the leg of a lass who fit Marta's description. The wound brought on a fever, and during her illness, she called out to her father over and over again, crying out, 'Nay, Father.' Once the woman healed, she and the man with her left and headed south. When Tor and Ainsley saw them in Berwick, they seemed comfortable with each other."

"Then we'll consider the feud over. I have no desire to force another marriage. You need to go back, my lady, and settle things with your brother. Only then should you two consider marriage. Hopefully by then Father Godfrey will have returned to the Highlands. I am done with this mess."

Royce stood and gave the king a deep bow. "Our thanks for yer audience and yer wisdom, Yer Majesty. The MacRobs are always at yer service."

"Be gone. My head is paining me over all you've told me."

Rhona stopped Royce when they reached the passageway and the door to the king's receiving room closed behind them. For the moment, they were alone.

She leaned toward him and whispered, "What do you suppose is happening with Father Godfrey?"

"I dinnae know, and I dinnae like it, lass. But we are both exhausted and will think better on it after a sound night's sleep." He led her down the passageway toward the steward's post, and the man summoned a footman to show them to

Rhona's bedchamber.

As they walked through the corridors, Rhona's mind went back to the earth-shattering news about the betrothal agreement, and she started to tremble. She barely heard Royce speaking to the footman, who'd opened a door and stood aside for them to enter.

"Many thanks to ye. The lady needs supper along with a bottle of wine."

The footman gave a small bow. "'Tis here now, my lord."

He motioned to someone in the passageway, and a serving lass entered and left a beautiful platter of food and a bottle of wine with two goblets. The two left and Royce closed the door.

Rhona saw a bed and nightstand, basin and ewer, on the far side of the room, and the table and chairs where their meal had been placed closer to the entrance. She took in no more than vague impressions of color. When she turned to Royce, the full force of their discovery hit her, and she fell against him, sobbing. Once or twice, she looked up at him and tried to speak, but she couldn't. What they'd learned was unspeakable.

After a quarter hour, Royce said, "Here now. I'll find ye a nice night rail and help ye undress. Then ye are going to eat and have a cup of wine. It will surely help ye to sleep."

"Royce, ye must stay with me. Please."

"Nay, no' until we are husband and wife. I'll speak with the steward in the morn and find a kirk where we can marry on the morrow. Then we must put the past behind us and live for our future together, lass."

He settled her at the table and opened a few drawers until he found a night rail. She stood, and Royce undid her ribbons. When she was free of bodice and skirt and the trews she'd worn for the ride, he blew out a tense breath. "Ye will test my control, Rhona, but I'll no' be in yer bed again until ye are officially mine."

She nodded, knowing he was doing the right thing. They were in the king's castle, after all. She kept her shift on and he helped her don the night rail. Then he settled her at the table, grabbing a fur from a basket by the hearth and wrapping it around her shoulders.

Her breath hitched as she did what she could to stop her tears. Royce set a trencher in front of her with a perfect-looking pear and thick slices of cheese on it.

She stared at the trencher. "You remember everything."

Pears had always been her favorite fruit. Four apples remained on the platter.

He'd chosen the pear for her.

"Of course I do. Ye'd eat a pear over an apple at every opportunity. Especially the ripe ones." He winked at her and grinned. "And I loved watching the juice dribble down yer chin."

She'd forgotten that. The man remembered their relationship better than she did, though she did recall a few of his preferences. "And you prefer meat over anything, but from tonight's choices, you'd pick the green apple over the red one."

He nodded, picked up the green apple, and sat next to her. He poured two goblets of wine. "Drink yer wine. 'Twill help ye sleep. I know ye have much on yer mind, but ye have to remember one thing."

"What?"

"We cannae change what happened. We must go forward. I know ye have to work it through yer mind, as I do. But we'll no' know the full truth until we can speak with yer brother. Until then, we should enjoy our time together, get married, and go home as husband and wife with the news that the feud is ended and King Alexander willnae force another marriage."

She leaned her head on his shoulder and said, "I missed you so much, Royce."

He always had a way of showing her the right of things.

"I missed ye too, love. But we are together now, and no one will tear us apart this time." He took another sip of his wine and stood. "Shall I tuck ye into yer bed?"

"Nay, because I'll tug you in with me." She giggled as if she were twenty again.

"Aye, ye're a wise one. If I go near ye, I fear I'll lose my control. Best if I settle myself outside the door. Lock the door from the inside. Do no' open it for anyone, understand?"

She followed him to the door. He gave her a quick kiss on the lips, then one to her cheek and her forehead. "Until the morrow, Rhona. Sleep well for our wedding day."

She closed and barred the door behind him and

sighed.

Everything would be wonderful from now on. For the rest of her life. She knew it.

CHAPTER TWELVE

ROYCE JERKED UP in the middle of the night, on his feet in a moment, his hand on the hilt of his sword. A guard jumped back and stood on the other side of the passageway, his hands held up in submission. "Sorry, my lord."

"Did ye awaken me apurpose?"

"Aye, the captain of the guard said ye need to see him right away."

Royce let go of his sword, then rubbed the sleep from his eyes. Sleeping on the floor in front of Rhona's door was only slightly better than sleeping on the ground in the cold.

"Why?" he asked quietly, hoping not to awaken Rhona.

"He has a message from yer brother. An urgent matter. He's just outside the side entrance, awaiting ye."

The guard disappeared in the opposite direction, and Royce stood in the middle of the deserted passageway. Should he tell Rhona he was leaving?

He looked up and down the passageway and stood listening for a long moment. There wasn't a soul about, and they were in the middle of the royal castle, guards everywhere. He knew her door was locked—he'd heard her turn the key after he'd left her.

She'd be fine.

The side entrance was a long way from Rhona's room—at least two corridors and a set of stairs before he even got outside—but guards kept watch throughout the castle.

Worrying about her was foolish. He just didn't like being away from her.

How his life had changed over the last moon. For the better.

He walked as quickly as possible, thinking about Father Godfrey, Ian and Marta, and the healers. He had a feeling the healers knew more than they were telling. And Father Godfrey was acting daft. Why?

He found a guard outside the side entrance, but they were the usual two guards assigned to that entrance, if he were to guess. He glanced around the area, searching for someone who looked like the captain of the guard, but saw no one.

The guard next to him turned and stared at him with a quizzical look. "May I help ye?"

"I was given a message that the captain of the guard is looking for me. He has an urgent message from my brother." Royce had a bad feeling deep in his gut. The kind that wouldn't go away.

"No' me nor anyone else has received any message."

"Is there a captain about?"

"Nay, no' at night. We've seen no unusual activity nor have we noticed anyone arriving at the stables. Ye must have it wrong."

"Did ye see the guard who just left the castle?"

The guard glanced around him. "No one has entered. The front entrance is locked at night. This is the only entrance and no one made it by us. Who are ye again?"

"MacRob. Laird of Clan MacRob."

He shook his head as confirmation. "Sorry."

Sudden alarm sent him flying back into the castle. Had it been a trick designed to get him away from Rhona? But why? Who would be interested in Rhona? And to risk hurting her or stealing her out of the king's own castle?

He skidded to a halt in the hallway outside her chamber. The door was open.

He stepped inside, not surprised to find it empty.

"Rhona?" he called out, the name echoing. It was a small chamber. He saw at a glance that she was gone.

He roared his fury, wanted to punch something, take the head off whoever had lured her out of safety, strike every palace guard who might have seen and saved her along the way.

He wrestled his anger back under control and looked around for any sign of who might have been there and what might have happened. The scarf she'd been wearing lay abandoned on the floor. He snatched it up and headed back outside. He'd seek out the guard who had woken him, then find Mungo, Struan, and Tamhas. He needed help. He had no idea where to look.

Rhona had been stolen.

This time he'd get her back.

~

Rhona awakened on a pallet in a darkened chamber. She had a fierce headache, and a large bump on her head to match. What the hell had happened?

At first, she could remember nothing about what had happened, but then, bit by bit, it started to come back to her. Someone had knocked on her door, and she opened it without thinking, expecting to see Royce. But the passageway had been empty. She must have stepped out of the room, because she'd been hit on the head before she could even register the presence of the man who'd jumped at her from the side.

Now, two sharp voices carried to her.

"Ye told me two gold coins."

"Take what I give ye. I didnae expect ye to nearly kill her. What if she never comes around? Will ye give me back the one coin?"

"Nay, she'll be fine. 'Tis a small bump, is all. Dinnae worry. But it was no' an easy thing to do. Those guards were difficult to draw away. And now the king's guards are all over Edinburgh looking for us. We'll no' be able to return for a few days."

"Then ye had better get away before ye are caught. If ye give my name to anyone, I'll find out and come for ye. I'll send the devil after ye."

Rhona controlled her gasp, her hands going to her mouth as if the man outside had just threatened her. Relieved that she could see a bit in the dark since her eyes were uncovered, she had a sudden understanding that the man who held her was a troubled one indeed.

Who was it?

CHAPTER THIRTEEN

ROYCE STOOD IN the open area in the center of the market with his guards, his arms crossed as he gave everything serious thought. There were too many places to look—he had to be smart about this search.

Mungo said, "I have nae idea who would want Rhona, but why no' go back and ask the king who is most likely to be disloyal?"

"I'll no' waste the time. I must go after her. We're in Edinburgh. He couldn't have gotten away without someone seeing him taking a woman through the city. She had to have been kept quiet somehow, or her yelling would have roused the city."

"There are many vegetable carts around for the marketplace. They could have hidden her under something in a cart."

"It happened in the middle of the night. There's no' much activity in the square at that time. People notice others making their way about, especially strangers. Someone would have noticed. I will tear Edinburgh apart if I must. I cannae lose her now."

Mungo clasped his shoulder and nodded to the

other two guards. "What next? I say we go back to the castle and question the staff, especially anyone in the stables and any guards who were on duty at the time."

"Ye and Tamhas do that," Royce said. "I'll take Struan to the market. The merchants are opening up, so mayhap someone saw something. We'll look for the drunks on the street, the ones who were still about at dawn."

"Ask everyone. Ye have nae idea who this is, if 'tis one person or a group. We'll question the guards again."

"I questioned everyone who was about this morn, and they all claimed ignorance, but perhaps ye'll get better answers than I will. After the market, I'll check inns, lodging houses, and taverns, anywhere a woman might be brought. Let's meet just outside the gate at high sun." He and Struan left, while Mungo and Tamhas headed in the opposite direction toward the castle. "She's no' far, Struan. I can feel it."

They headed toward the center of the burgh, his mind wandering to the past. What was and what should have been . . .

~

Thirteen years ago . . .

Royce snickered, glancing over at Broden Shaw in his green and black plaid, the kind that stood out easily.

Next to him, Adair asked, "Why are ye laughing?

Ye havenae won yet."

"Look at Shaw. He thinks he'll win everything, just as he always does. I'm going to beat his arse this year."

Adair and Tor looked at Royce's competition. "His best event is the obstacle course. His stallion is one fine beast, and he rides like he was born to it," Adair said. "Ye're good, but he's better."

"But I can beat him at archery."

"True," Tor said. "Ye're the best archer in the whole of Scotland. They say Struan will best ye someday."

"Someday is no' this day." Something caught his eye. "Who is that?" Royce asked, seeing a new contender enter the lineup as they waited for the signal to ready themselves and their horses.

"Never seen him before. I dinnae recognize the plaid."

"Someone said 'tis a cousin of Shaw's. He's young."

"Young!" Royce grinned. "Adair, ye and Tor are both taller than him. He's small."

"Ye'll beat him easily."

"I only care about Broden."

A horn sounded, and Tor said, "There's the signal. Mount up, brother. Beat his arse! Mayhap I'll trip him in the forest."

"Ye do, and I'll skin yer hide. I'll beat him fair. I dinnae need yer help." Royce knew he would win.

Broden gave him one last look, a wide smile on his face, then the flag dropped to start the race. Royce's stallion burst off the starting line and down the course, and he took the lead easily.

The course's multiple jumps, sharp turns, and other obstacles would challenge horse and rider both, ending in a race through thick forest to the finish line.

But Royce was distracted. The cousin no one knew somehow managed to end up directly behind him, and he had no idea how he'd done it. How he wished he could have watched him. The only thing that struck him was that the rider was small, so the horse could move faster with less weight on its back.

Could it make that much of a difference?

He wouldn't let the fool beat him. He was going to win and lord it over Broden Shaw for the whole next year. He was tired of the man's gloating over last year's results. The title of the greatest rider would go to Royce.

Royce MacRob. He'd make his sire proud, and all the Shaws would be envious. The two clans were allies—he and his siblings had played with the Shaws when they were younger and still counted each other friends. And rivals. As they'd grown up, their rivalry had grown fiercer and fiercer.

And no one was more competitive than Royce.

He managed to get ahead of the Shaw rider, and he never looked back to see where Broden was. He was far enough in the lead that he didn't need to worry. He would finish far ahead.

They entered the forest, the change from bright sun to forest gloom so noticeable that the horses slowed for a few strides. But Royce had practiced this with his stallion many times, so the animal recovered quickly and raced on, almost to the finish line.

Here, the race hinged on strategy more than skill in overcoming obstacles. The course of the race split, giving each rider a choice of three different paths through the forest. Broden would take the path on the right, but Royce knew the course in the center to be the best.

To his surprise, from the path on the left came that blasted unknown rider, managing to bring his mount directly in front of Royce. That was impossible. Royce and Adair had tried it many times. The path on the left was the slowest. Even Broden hadn't taken it.

But the wee fool landed directly in front of him, wearing a strange teal-colored plaid, making a deliberate bid to slow Royce's horse. To make him lose.

The horse slowed, and Royce couldn't get around it on the narrow path. He urged his horse as close to the other as possible, nose almost touching the other horse's tail.

Who was this rider? He looked more closely, hoping he might recognize him, and then something caught his attention. Something he didn't like.

The rider's arse was quite delectable.

"Hellfire, ye'll no' make me lose, whoever ye are."

The horse ahead of him slowed still more, and he caught sight of Broden's horse flying ahead on the adjacent path, and to his surprise a fourth horse managed to get ahead of all of them, moving too quickly for him to see who it was.

He lost his temper, so angry with this wee trickster in front of him that he would knock him off his horse to take him out of the race. They reached a clearing wide enough for him to pull abreast of him, and Royce reached over and pushed the rider's shoulder, but the fool held on. Royce tried again, giving a huge shove, enough to send him flying off his mount, but the stubborn arse grabbed Royce's tunic and held on, knocking them both off balance.

They tumbled together, their horses bolting. Royce somersaulted arse over head and landed right next to the fool. He rolled over and pinned the lad to the ground, ready for a fight.

At the last second, he stopped, his fist hanging in midair. He knew those wide eyes, that laughing mouth.

"Rhona?"

CHAPTER FOURTEEN

RHONA LAY CURLED into a ball against the cold in the chamber where she'd awoken. She couldn't help but think of her dear daughter and wonder how she was doing without her. Annie was her whole world, and she'd just agreed to welcome Royce into that world. But now this. What else could happen?

The arguing had stopped a few minutes ago, and now she heard shuffling, footsteps, and a door closing. It sounded as though two people left. She was—she prayed—alone.

Time to work on her escape.

Pushing up from the pallet, she smoothed her night rail and brushed her hair out of her eyes. With a deep breath, she moved over to the door and tested the handle.

It didn't budge.

She slammed the door with the heel of her hand in frustration. She couldn't blame her kidnapper. It was the only way to keep her here. Her first reaction was to claw at the door, and then to tug as hard as she could. Finally she had to admit the uselessness of her efforts, and she turned to survey the room, though there wasn't much to look at. It appeared to have been empty for a long time, mayhap a year or more, judging by the thick layer of dust on everything. One chest and a chair were the only other furniture. There was a small window, too small for her to climb out, but she pulled the shutter back to peer outside.

Nothing but forest greeted her eyes. She had no clue as to where she was being held, though she had to guess she was still near Edinburgh.

She prayed she was still near Edinburgh. Royce would never find her if she was anywhere else.

She found the clothes she'd worn the day before tossed on the floor, so she put them on. Her assailant must have grabbed them before he carried her out.

Of that, at least, she was grateful. If she had the chance, she'd run, and she'd much rather be dressed.

A dark foreboding filled her as she glanced around the room. The small room. Not much more than a closet. She did not like confined spaces. Small spaces. The kind that made you think you were a prisoner.

She had to get out. Had to.

"Royce," she whispered, wondering what he'd thought when he'd discovered her missing.

She sank onto the bed and lay down to save her strength. He would come for her. Surely he would. She'd always drawn his attention.

~

Thirteen years ago

She would trick him into anger. If that was the only way she could get him to notice her, then so be it.

She'd watched him from afar forever—at least six moons. She was ten and nine summers old, and it was time to choose a husband, her mother and father kept telling her.

She'd chosen Royce. Now she just had to get him to pick her in return.

Having planned this long ago, she knew which path to take. Being a lass, she was a much lighter weight on her mount, and the stablemaster had helped her train her horse for two moons. She had to get her horse ahead of him, just because she knew it would infuriate him. Spitting mad, he'd knocked her off her horse, but she grabbed on to him, pulling him to the ground with her.

She knew exactly what would happen, and it did.

He pinned her and was about to throw his first punch when she reached up and yanked her cap off to reveal a head full of curls. She laughed at his shocked face.

"Rhona?"

She arched her brow at him.

He glared at her, but then asked, "Why would ye . . . why . . . why . . . ?"

She reached for him, setting her hand on the back of his neck and tugging his face down to hers. "This is why. Ye ignore me, and I dinnae like it."

She set her lips against his, and to her delight, he kissed her back. She'd feared failure, that he would decide to pummel her after all, but she should have known better. He would never pummel her.

It was almost as if the lightning in a dark sky struck them both, fusing their souls.

She'd known it. They belonged together. The universe and the stars said so.

And so did she.

She kissed him, and his response was more than she ever would have expected. He didn't just kiss her, he ravaged her. At first, his lips were gentle, but then his passion took over and he plundered her mouth with his tongue until they were both gasping, the heat between them reaching her belly.

It had been the only way she could get him to notice her.

It had worked.

Their kiss seemed to last forever, and she felt his hardness press between her legs. His hand went to her breast, cupping her through the fabric, and when he pinched her nipple, she squealed into his mouth, arching against him in search of a completion she hadn't known she'd needed.

He ended the kiss as quickly as she'd started it.

"Lass, if ye wanted me, all ye had to do was ask."

"I want ye."

He smiled and pushed himself off her, then held his hand out to her. "Ye are lucky this was a fine distraction. I wouldnae lose first place for many."

"But ye will for me?" She took his hand and let him pull her to her feet.

"I would do aught for ye, Rhona. Just ask."

They caught their horses and rode together to the finish line—last in the race, but with a much finer prize. When Tor and Adair asked him what had happened to him during the race, Rhona smiled and said, "He met me."

The way he looked at her melted her heart.

Rhona remembered the day as if it had been yesterday. She'd been kept home, away from the MacRobs, for a time that year, and when she'd laid eyes on Royce again, she nearly swooned. The baby-faced eldest son had turned into a handsome man who stole her heart with his beautiful smile. Even his occasional scruffy beard had appealed to her. He had a way of looking at her that told her she was the only thing that mattered to him.

How she wished he would look at her that way again.

He'd proposed marriage to her—sort of—but she hadn't accepted. But then she sort of had, during their audience with the king. She wasn't sure why she hadn't immediately accepted his offer, especially since it had been her idea in the first place. She couldn't blame him for his time with Louisa. She was surprised he hadn't married another, in fact. Hell, expecting the man to live without taking care of his needs was ridiculous. It had been twelve years.

Thinking about their time together had lodged a wanting inside her that no one but he could quell. If he was anything like her, he had to be feeling the same. She'd sensed it—felt it against her backside—when they'd lain together in their camp two days ago.

The music their lovemaking created couldn't possibly be replicated with any other person.

It belonged to them and only them.

She needed Royce MacRob, her protector, her lover and, she hoped, soon her husband.

Tears pricked her eyes, but she refused to give in. Somewhere, a door slammed, and she jerked up from the pallet. Was it the same man?

She heard a key in the lock of her door, so she stood, backing up to the opposite wall. Should she run at him, try to knock him down?

The door opened and she gasped.

"What the hell?"

CHAPTER FIFTEEN

ROYCE MADE HIS way through one side of the market while Struan worked his way through the opposite side, asking everyone, every merchant, customer, and vagrant if they'd seen Rhona in the wee hours of the morning. Every once in a while, he would look at Struan and lift his chin in question. Struan always shook his head in denial.

He was getting nowhere too.

He looked down the street, hoping he might see Rhona strolling toward him. Nay, it was not her but he thought he caught sight of someone he knew.

The healers from the morning before. And they were coming toward him.

He called out, "Odart!"

The two stopped and exchanged a frightened look, but then Odart faced him, pushing Eufemie behind him. She looked like she was about to break into tears.

"What do ye want?" Odart asked, standing in front of his wife, his chin raised.

"Have ye seen Rhona? She was stolen out of the castle in the middle of the night, and I have no idea who would do such a thing. She was taken from me."

Eufemie let out a little cry behind Odart, and Royce turned his gaze to her. She would not meet it.

"Eufemie? What is it ye arenae telling me?"

"Naught," Odart replied, giving a harsh tug on his wife's arm.

"Ye always act like that toward yer wife?"

"We dinnae know where Rhona is."

Struan came up behind the pair and unsheathed his sword, which Royce hoped would frighten Eufemie into telling them what she knew.

Odart tried to turn and walk away from them, but Struan blocked them, and the older man halted. Eufemie wrung her hands but didn't move otherwise.

Royce pointed to a spot away from the busy marketplace. "Over there, Struan. I'll talk to Eufemie there."

They made their way over to the quiet corner Royce had indicated, but Odart was still upset. "We dinnae know aught. Ye have nae right to keep us here."

Royce rested his hand on the hilt of his sword. He worried that if he made more threats, the healer would clam up completely, so he tried to gentle his voice. "Eufemie, tell us what ye know."

Eufemie looked at her husband, who shook his head furiously.

"I cannae lie, Odart. Forgive me, but I had no idea it was Rhona he was after."

"Who?" Royce said loud enough to make

Eufemie jump.

"Dinnae speak to my wife so, be ye laird or no'." Odart again moved between Royce and his wife.

"My apologies, Eufemie. Kindly tell us what ye know." He took a step back and waited.

Eufemie's tears slid down her cheeks when she answered. "We didnae know it was Rhona." Odart cursed and turned away from her, but he didn't go far. "The priest caught up to us no' long after we parted from yer company. He was pleased to see us and said the Lord needed us to do a favor for him. I didnae wish to do it, but he threatened us, said the devil would strike us down. He wanted us to distract the castle guards inside so he and his serving man could get by without their notice. He offered us silver, my lord, and we need it badly. We only wished to help, but what a mess it has become."

"Eufemie," Royce whispered, wanting the part she was holding back. "Exactly what did ye do for the coin?"

"We distracted the guards so he and his man could go down the passageway and then return, and we saw the other man carrying a lass over his shoulder, saw the wavy hair, but we didnae see her face. After hearing yer tale, it must have been Rhona. But we didnae know what he was doing. We would have never guessed he wished to take Rhona captive. We thought ye two were together. Why would he want Rhona? All he kept telling us was he had to save Marta from Ian."

Her eyes pleaded with him, and his heart went

out to her.

Whoever stole Rhona had surprised many.

"Where did he take her?" He wished to wring Odart's neck, but clearly they had not understood their true part in this catastrophe.

"I dinnae know. He didnae tell us his purpose or plan."

"Who? Who stole her away?"

He couldn't have been more surprised by their answer.

"Father Godfrey."

~

"Father Godfrey, why are you here?" Rhona asked. Then the truth dawned on her. *He* had taken her from the castle. She was sure of it. But why?

He grabbed her by the arm, pinching the tender skin of her underarm as he yanked her over to the table. "I'll tell ye why. Because yer lies could get me in trouble. Ye will go with me to King Alexander and recant everything ye told him about me being in Berwick. If he finds out I am the one who injured Marta, he could have me defrocked. I thought Ian was going to hurt her. That was all. He pulled a knife, and I tried to stop him, but Marta got hurt. 'Twas no' my fault."

"Father, I think you'd better tell me your side of the story." Maybe if she could get him talking, she might unravel a bit of this puzzle. Or distract him so she could escape.

"I was trying to save Marta. And no one knew

what Ian was going to do with her. I feared for her life, so I confronted them. That's when Marta was hurt. I took her to the healer, then went back after Ian, but he was gone. He must have found the healers and hidden there. I saw Tor and Ainsley riding away and talking about searching for Ian and Marta, so I followed them.

"I never saw Bishop Timlin. I was trying to save a lass who was in serious danger, and ye've twisted my honest efforts into something they are no'. Why did ye tell the king I was in Berwick?"

"Because Tor . . . wait . . . how do you know what we told the king? No one else was in the room, certainly not you. How did you know?"

"Because I followed ye too. I thought Tor and Ainsley told ye where to find Ian and Marta, so I followed ye when ye left. I didnae know ye were going to the king. I thought ye were just going after Marta and Ian. I have to know she is safe! I heard ye talking to the healers. Marta was talking about her father, no' me. She wanted someone to get her father to help her. 'Tis exactly what she was saying. But he wasnae there, so I helped. I *helped*!"

Something was not right about his story. The healers hadn't said anything about Father Godfrey bringing Marta to them. They'd said the couple had come together. What was this priest about?

Perhaps it would be best if she decided to appease the man. "Well, I'm sure no one would suspect anything else of you, Father. You are a priest and wouldn't hurt even an ant crawling across the floor. We all know you have a good heart."

He grinned. "Of course. How do ye think I was able to get into the castle without any trouble? No one questions a priest. But I am still concerned that ye said I was seen in Berwick. Ye have to go tell the king that Ainsley said they were mistaken. That I was never there. Ye will agree to go with me, aye?"

Rhona's instinct was to refuse him. She wasn't about to lie to her monarch, but then she realized that agreeing to see King Alexander could get her into the castle, where she stood a better chance of rescue or escape. Or if she were out in the streets of the burgh, any of the guards might see her. And if not and they did get an audience with the king, Godfrey could not stop her from telling the truth.

She would go along with Godfrey long enough to get out of this hut and into the streets of Edinburgh. One good scream, and someone would see her, find her, get her help. She could not stay in this locked chamber a moment longer.

It was too much like that hated room in MacAdder's castle.

"Understood. I'll do whatever you wish, Father."

"Verra wise, Lady MacAdder."

She shuddered at the name, like she always did, but she said nothing. She had a thousand questions for the priest, but she would bite her tongue until they were outside, for fear he'd change his mind.

He tossed a mantle at her, and she put it on. While Father Godfrey wasn't anywhere near the size of her brother or Royce, he was still taller than her. She doubted she could fight him off on her own. She might be able to outrun him, but there was no point in trying until she knew exactly where she was.

Get on the horse and head to the castle, Rhona. Then you can get away. You have to. For Annie. You are all she has.

The thought of her daughter gave her strength, banished her fear. She thanked the Lord that she'd introduced Annie to her aunt and uncle and to Tor. Ainsley would take care of her daughter if she didn't make it back. She'd grow up to be a strong, beautiful lass, surrounded by loving family. But she *would* make it back.

Forcing herself not to think on the worst, she followed the priest out of the cottage, then moved over to the horse he pointed out to her, a fine mount that seemed well fed. He held the reins while she mounted the horse from the rock.

"Give me yer hands," Godfrey ordered. She held them out, and he forced them together, tying her wrists quickly with a short length of coarse rope. When he was satisfied, he pulled her mantle over her hands so no one would notice.

He mounted behind her and kneed the horse into motion. Rhona sat motionless and silent as they rode away from the hut, and for a quarter hour, she saw nothing she recognized. Finally, they turned onto the main road into Edinburgh. Still, there were too few people about for her to attempt to get help. She would pay attention to her surroundings in case she managed to get away, but it would be better to wait until they reached the burgh proper, where Royce and their guards would surely be searching for her.

The traffic on the road increased as they grew closer to Edinburgh, but Rhona recognized no one. Father Godfrey played his part well with murmurs of "Blessings on ye all" and "Please allow us by so we may do the work of the Lord."

He held something sharp against her back whenever they were close to others. While she couldn't believe he'd actually hold a knife against her, she wished to say he didn't need to. She wouldn't do anything until they arrived safely in Edinburgh. She'd say nothing, knowing strangers would believe the priest over her if she tried to call for aid.

When the burgh came into sight, she asked, "Why did you go to Berwick?"

"I told ye that I went to save Marta. Why else would I go there?"

"Did you find her? Are Marta and Ian hale?"

"Nay."

"Nay, you did not find her, or nay, they are not hale?"

"Never mind. We're moving into town."

"Please tell me they are well, and I'll be quiet, Father." It had been more than a sennight since Tor and Ainsley had seen the pair in Berwick. If Father Godfrey had more recent news of them, she needed him to tell her.

"Marta and Ian are dead."

"I don't believe you! You're lying just to get me to do what you want." She wished to slap the smirk off his face. "Father Godfrey, what has happened to you? Please tell me. Why are you behaving so strangely?"

"My business is my own, and none of yers nor the king's. I went to save her, but the two were dead and I dinnae know how. Mayhap Marta and Ian were killed by reivers. I learned of their deaths near the harbor. I think he was trying to take her to France and she fought him. He probably killed her and then took his own life."

Rhona didn't know what to say. Could it be true?

This Father Godfrey was not the priest she knew who had taken such good care of so many on Shaw and MacRob land. He'd turned daft, of that much she was sure, but how was she to find out if he was being truthful?

She needed Royce.

They entered Edinburgh but turned away from the central square and marketplace, avoiding the vendors and crowds. She ground her teeth in frustration. She'd hoped he'd go down the main thoroughfare. It didn't matter. If she saw one MacRob or Shaw plaid, she'd do her best to get their attention.

"Dinnae try aught foolish, Rhona. If ye try to run, I'll catch ye easily, even if ye managed to get to the ground without falling. There is no one here to save ye. No one knows or cares about Rhona MacAdder. The king will lock ye up for the lies ye've told. I've always been a favorite of his. Once I see him and ye recant yer story, all will be well."

She waited and waited . . . and waited . . .

Down one street, and then another, and a third street. Finally, though, Father Godfrey could avoid the main road no longer—it was the only one that went up the hill to the castle. She glanced down both ways, and toward the far end below them, she saw exactly what she'd hoped for—a MacRob plaid, that glorious shade of blue with threads of white that stood out so strong against the others. She'd know it anywhere, even from any distance.

She yelled the loudest way possible. "Royce! Help me!"

CHAPTER SIXTEEN

Twelve and a half years ago

ROYCE LEANED AGAINST the tree, their tree since he'd engraved their initials on it, and grinned. She was off hiding again—the wee minx was quite a tease. They played this game often, and it always ended with the very best loving between them.

He'd just as soon skip it and go straight to no clothes and a bed. Finish in a quarter hour with a loud grunt. Their mating was magnificent.

But Rhona had the oddest sense of foreplay.

If someone had told him a year ago that he would be madly in love with Rhona Shaw, he would have laughed and walked away. But there was no denying the powerful attraction they had for each other or the power of their love.

He had indeed said the word and meant it.

He didn't ever want a life without Rhona in it. He would ask for her hand when her sire recovered from his illness. For sure he would accept him, and they'd marry quickly. The poor man had a fever, but he would surely get better soon.

"Rhona, love, where are ye?" He rolled his eyes, wondering where she could be hiding this time. She never ceased to surprise him.

Once she'd been sitting on a log with her breasts fully exposed and cupped in her own hands. When he'd set his eyes on her, she'd rubbed her thumbs over her nipples. He'd never turned hard so fast in his life, and nearly finished as he watched her.

He'd picked her up, making her squeal, and made love to her against a tree, though he'd been forced to apologize many times for being so rough. She'd claimed to love every moment of it, and if the sound of her climax was any indication, he had to agree. He'd wanted to carve their initials in the tree he'd held her against, but she'd refused to allow it, saying it should be left unspoiled as proof of its value.

He'd chuckled and said, "Whatever pleases my wee nymph." And he'd chosen a different tree to carve, the one he leaned against now.

Then there was the time she'd played the game and stripped down to nothing, sitting on a soft cushion of moss, only to find herself with a rash on her sweet bottom. He'd kissed every spot on her round cheeks.

She'd squealed from that too. That was when he'd introduced her to the joys of his tongue on her nether region.

He couldn't help but chuckle thinking of the time she'd hidden behind a tree, her sweet arse a bit wider than the trunk of the tree. When a group of hunters came through the trees, she'd run away, hiding behind him while she quickly dressed. It had been her brother. Fortunately, they'd been a good distance away when he'd spotted them and warned her.

She'd nearly died of embarrassment.

The lass was so bold for one so young, and he loved it.

He tipped his head back and stared up at the gray sky, wishing the sun would come out and warm the area a bit. Autumn could be too cold.

Out of nowhere he heard her yell. And this one wasn't teasing. It was real.

"Rhona! Where are ye?" He chased the sound of her voice through the trees to find her caught in a tight thicket of trees and undergrowth, fighting to get out. She'd managed to get herself thoroughly tangled by a whippy sapling and a snarl of brambles.

"Help me, Royce. I'm stuck. I cannae get out. I dinnae like being in such a close area. Get me out. Please hurry."

Her tears ripped at his heart, and he ripped cuts and gouges in his hands getting her out. She threw herself into his arms, trembling with fear.

"I hate close spaces."

"Love, then dinnae climb into them," he suggested, but that earned him a quick swat on his upper arm.

~

Now that Royce had Rhona back, the thought of losing her again pushed panic into his throat.

He shoved it back down. MacAdder had torn her from his arms once. He'd let no one else do it now.

Mungo and Struan had joined him quickly, learning nothing from anyone at the castle.

He headed back up the street, looking in every direction possible, running into people and market stalls as he went. He cursed himself for not being able to figure out where Father Godfrey could be holding her.

He barked at Struan and Mungo, "Meet over there." He pointed off to the side.

Once they'd gathered, Tamhas joining them, he said, "We have to go out of the burgh. She's no' here. I dinnae care what that seer in the booth told ye, Mungo."

His second had foolishly paid a seer for information, but she'd said they'd find Rhona on the street.

After wasting half the hour looking for her, Royce was ready to move on.

"I agree," Mungo said. "Tamhas, go get our mounts ready. I'll grab a few meat pies for us. We've no' eaten since last eve. Let's meet back here."

Those two set off in separate directions. Royce stepped back into the street for one final pass. Then he heard it.

Her yell. He'd know that yell anywhere— exactly as it had been back in the forest so many years ago.

"Rhona! Scream again!" His bellow scared everyone near him, which conveniently opened up the street.

Mungo came sprinting back from his errand.

"Where?" he asked.

She called his name out, the most blessed sound he'd heard in a long time. Then he saw her on a horse halfway up the road to the castle, Father Godfrey riding double behind her. He pointed, hoping his guards took note, and broke into a dead run up the road.

He was going to kill the bastard, priest or not.

"Let her go, Godfrey!"

He ran straight at him, and even though the priest kicked at the horse's flank, the animal only tossed its head and whinnied, unable to get through the market crowd with any speed. But neither could Royce move fast enough to catch up.

"Royce, help! My hands are tied." She glanced back over her shoulder, the fear on her face evident.

He chased them all the way to the entrance to the castle, and he thought his lungs would explode before he reached the top of the hill. Blasted Edinburgh Castle was too high up.

But the horse was more hampered, carrying two riders and unable to duck and dodge as Royce could. Right outside the gate, he launched himself at Father Godfrey, knocking the fool clear off the horse. A roar of protests rose from the watching crowd.

"He's a priest!"

"Dinnae hurt a man of God."

"Leave the priest be."

"Get him! He's hurting a priest."

Royce grabbed Father Godfrey by the neck, hauling him off the ground and ripping his collar off. "He's no' a true priest. He's a demon."

That didn't stop a group of men circling him, and members of the king's guard marched out from the gate to see what the disturbance was about.

Royce called out to Mungo, who was just reaching the top of the hill. "Mungo, get Rhona!"

Mungo saluted an acknowledgment and angled toward the confused horse and its rider trying to manage the loose reins with bound hands.

Struan and Tamhas joined Royce, swords in hand. Royce had drawn his dagger and had it held against Godfrey's side.

"He's a kidnapper and a liar. The king will decide what becomes of him."

Just at that moment, the castle guards arrived, and the crowd backed off slowly as a group, giving Royce space to move.

"Let me go, MacRob," Godfrey hissed through clenched teeth.

Mungo approached with Rhona, but Royce could spare her no more than a glance. She looked fine, though she rubbed at her wrists, and he prayed Godfrey had not hurt her.

"The hell I will. No one touches Rhona, Godfrey. Rhona, are ye hale?" He managed to hold the priest with one arm while he held the other one out to Rhona. She flew into his arms with a whimper. "Ye are hale? Tell me he didnae hurt ye." He kissed her forehead and glanced over her, looking for any sign of blood.

"I'm fine, Royce, but I don't believe he is who he claims to be. He kept saying he was just trying to save Marta, but I don't know that I believe him. His heart is twisted." She lifted her chin and glared at Father Godfrey, then leaned her head onto Royce's shoulder.

"MacRob, I was just trying to protect a lass of yer clan. Ian was after her. He wished to kill her. I couldnae allow that to happen."

Royce was so upset, he could hardly listen to the man. He didn't know what to believe after all he'd heard.

"Rhona, ye promised to recant yer story," Godfrey whined.

"Nay, I did not. You ordered me to, but I did *not* agree."

Royce kissed her again and explained, "I have to let ye go so I can handle this scum in my other hand. Walk with Struan and Tamhas." She did as he said, and he led his group to the castle guards. "I am Laird Royce MacRob, and this piece of dung who claims to be a priest kidnapped Lady Rhona Shaw. He must face the king's justice."

"Ye dinnae know what ye're talking about, MacRob!" Godfrey protested. "I am one of the king's favorites, and I was only trying to save a lass in yer clan. I tell ye Ian wished to kill her." The priest squirmed in his grasp, and Royce was two whispers away from kicking him square in his bollocks.

Priest. Royce was more deserving of priesthood than this bastard.

"I've heard enough from yer foul mouth," he said, turning Godfrey to face him with the strength of one hand. Then he pulled his fist back and hit the priest square in the jaw.

Godfrey cowered and rubbed his jaw. "Arrest him for striking a man of the cloth," he said feebly.

"That man kidnapped me," Rhona said, stepping to Royce's side. "He knocked me out and stole me out of the king's castle."

The captain of the guard nodded. "Aye, we've been searching for ye all this morn, my lady. Come this way, please." He turned to one of his men. "Inform the king what has happened and get everyone else away from here."

The guard hurried off, and the captain turned back to Royce. "If ye dinnae mind, we'll await the king's orders. We'll take this man under guard for ye, my lord. He's in the king's custody now."

Royce nodded once and passed Godfrey over to the guards. They circled him, swords at the ready.

It seemed like forever before the king came out the door, guards flanking him, but Royce suspected it hadn't been nearly as long as it felt.

"What now, MacRob?"

"What now? Excuse me, Yer Majesty, but did ye no' hear that Rhona was kidnapped right out of yer castle? Yer guards paid no attention to the abductor because it was Father Godfrey. 'Tis exactly how the evil man got past everyone. He didnae expect to be questioned. But he needed help so he could get her out without being stopped. Someone distracted yer guards so the priest could get her out the door without prying eyes." Royce clenched his fists at his sides to stop himself from stealing Godfrey back from the guards and choking him.

The king moved over to stand in front of Father Godfrey, who still clutched his jaw, but he could use it well enough to complain about Royce. Pointing at him, he whined, "He hit me. Twice. A priest. And all I've done is try to save a lass of the MacRob clan from an evil man trying to take her life. 'Tis an honorable cause. I had a good reason to be in Berwick."

"Get up, Father. Rhona MacAdder, is it true that this man accosted you and removed you from my castle against your will?"

"Aye, Your Majesty. I was sleeping. Someone knocked and when I opened the door, I was hit over the head. I still have the bump to prove it." She bent her head toward the king, but he waved for her to straighten.

"Never mind. I believe you. You have no reason to lie, while this man does. Father Godfrey, this is the second time I've heard of you causing trouble. You will stay under guard for now and will perform no duties of a priest until I speak with the bishop. Guards, lock him up until the bishop arrives."

"Please, Yer Majesty. I've done naught wrong!" Father Godfrey cried. "Saving a lass is hardly a reason for being locked up!"

"Naught wrong?" Royce said. "Ye stole the lass I'm in love with. Dinnae say ye've done naught wrong." He wanted to choke the lies out of the other man's mouth.

"MacRob!" the king chided. "Quiet. I'll hear from you in a moment. Father Godfrey, the more you beg the worse it will be for you. Take him away."

Once Godfrey was removed, the king faced Royce. "Are you finished yelling at a man of the cloth? Until the bishop defrocks him, he's still a priest to you."

"No' yet," Royce grumbled. He got down on one knee in front of Rhona and asked, "Rhona, will ye marry me here and now, please? We can marry here and go home as husband and wife. I cannae stand the thought of no' having ye by my side for the rest of our days. Mayhap 'tis no' so romantic, but 'tis because I love ye and my soul needs ye nearby."

Rhona stared at him, then looked to King Alexander.

The king clasped his hands in front of him and said, "I think by now you know the man loves you. Look what he did for you."

"Nay," she said, tears coming down her cheeks. "I mean, you must answer a question for me first, Royce. It has been bothering me terribly."

"What?" the king asked. "You are as daft as the priest."

"What is this about, Rhona?" Royce thought they'd settled everything. He thought she loved him. He didn't know what to do, but his heart had just been ripped in two again. "And ye cry too? Do ye hate me so much? Whatever ye wish to ask I'll gladly answer."

"I know it makes no sense to you, but it's important to me. I cannot love a man who has forgotten so much of our relationship."

The king shook his head and stepped away, giving them a bit of privacy.

"What did I forget? I recall everything, I'm sure, though I'd no' like to explain it all to ye in front of an audience."

She swiped the tears from her cheeks, and they were slowing, but she had a determined expression he didn't like. He recalled that look well, and always before it meant her stubbornness was digging in for a fight.

She swallowed hard and lifted her chin. "You forgot something important to me, and it made me question your dedication. You are not the man I thought you were if you could forget such a thing." She gazed up at him, and he could see in her eyes just how hurt she was.

"What did I forget?"

She mumbled, "You forgot our tree."

Her lower lip quivered so badly, he had to put an end to her torture.

He had to choke down his laughter, but instead moved over, cupped her face and brushed her tears away with his thumbs, then said, "Nay, I didnae forget. How could I?"

"But you said I was daft before," she whimpered, her eyes now all red.

"The tree? What about the tree?" King Alexander asked, looking from one to the next.

"He forgot!" She crossed her arms and set her mouth. He had to fight to keep from laughing at her beloved, beautiful, fearsome expression. And because he knew the truth.

"I didnae forget, Rhona." He leaned down and whispered, "Ye had the wrong tree, love."

"What?" Her eyes widened.

"Ye were pointing to the tree that I carved our initials on. That wasnae the same tree. Ye would no' allow me to carve my initials on *our* tree."

She thought for a moment, and he could tell when she realized her mistake. She broke into a wide grin and threw herself at him with a squeal. "You are right. *I* forgot. Our tree was a different tree." She kissed him, then said, "Aye, I'll marry you, Royce MacRob, and let's do it quickly. I do not wish to wait until we go home."

"What does the tree have to do with it?" the king asked, his hands on his hips.

The two looked at him and shouted in unison, "Never mind!"

Rhona, looking quite sheepish, whispered, "Never mind, if you please, Your Majesty."

CHAPTER SEVENTEEN

SEVEN PEOPLE GATHERED outside the castle chapel that night, including the king's priest, Rhona, and Royce. Mungo, Struan, Tamhas, and King Alexander himself would serve as witnesses.

The king offered his arm to Rhona and asked, "May I escort you inside, my dear?"

"I'd be honored, Your Majesty." She smiled, feeling like a princess. One of his housemaids had brought her a lovely gown of deep blue velvet, and it fit her perfectly.

"Now you may tell your brother that not only do I support your marriage, I witnessed it."

"He'll be honored you did. I am honored."

The ceremony was simple, but Rhona couldn't be happier. The dream she'd held on to for years had come true. Her only regret was that Ainsley and Annie weren't there. She could not wait to bring them the news.

She still would not have welcomed her brother, though. Why had he not investigated the agreement that MacAdder had produced?

She put it out of her mind for now—she would not allow her lingering anger with Broden to ruin her wedding day.

Rhona didn't hear a word the priest said until she had to say, "Aye." She was so pleased to be on Royce's arm, standing next to him at the altar and finally marrying him that she couldn't listen.

No man would ever abuse her again.

She deserved this happiness—had deserved it all along.

After the ceremony, the king kissed her on both cheeks, clapped Royce on the shoulder in congratulations, then returned to his duties. She and Royce and their guards ate a quiet dinner in a private hall. The kitchen must have been told it was a wedding feast, because the table was laden with roast lamb, meat pies, loaves of dark bread, peas and carrots, and a luscious honey-sweet apple dish.

But Rhona wished to be alone with her husband.

Royce seemed to share her desire. He ate a bite of this and a bite of that, but his attention drifted to her more often than the food. Before long, he rose and said, "Gentlemen, enjoy yer meal. We'll see ye out front on the morrow to start our journey back to MacRob land. Until then."

Mungo called out after him, "Dinnae forget where ye are, MacRob."

"What did he mean by that, Royce?" Rhona whispered.

"Dinnae know and dinnae care. Mungo likes to tease. I'll no' let him distract me from my fine new wife."

He ushered her into the passageway, and they were greeted by a housemaid. "This way please, my lord and lady. Yer bedchamber is ready."

The bedchamber held the most luxurious bed Rhona had ever seen. Adorned with gold curtains held back by braided ties, the bed had a dark red silk coverlet and several tufted pillows of varying shades of gold and black. The hearth had a blazing fire already, two chairs in front with a table between. There were various chests and sconces holding candles, but the atmosphere was cozy and private. Apparently, Royce felt the same, as she heard him give the same wee gasp she did.

"We took the liberty of preparing a bath for ye, my lady," the housemaid said, gesturing toward a curtained alcove. "I'll be pleased to attend ye while ye bathe."

"Thank ye for yer kindness, but we'll no' need ye this night," Royce said. "I'll tend my wife."

The woman blushed, bowed, and left.

"Now I have ye to myself. Finally."

"Not until I have my bath, Royce. Please." She backed up, and he followed her.

"Oh, I dinnae think so, wife of mine. I'd be pleased to help ye undress and wash yer hard-to-reach places."

She placed her hand on his chest. "Royce, you did not see where I was held by Father Godfrey. I feel so dirty. Please? I know you're anxious, but grant me a wee bit of time to soak. I need to let it all leave my body. Wash it away."

His eyes turned dark, and she wasn't sure if it was fury or desire, but he lifted her hand and kissed each knuckle. "Aye, of course, my love. Forgive me for being thoughtless."

"You are not thoughtless. It was a difficult day, but I'm very happy now, and full of joy to be married to you. But the tub is what I wish for first."

"Go ahead, lass. I'll have a goblet of wine while ye bathe. I'll no' rest if I walk out that door for fear another daft man will steal ye away from me."

"That suits me perfectly." She stepped around the curtain, not surprised to see the large wooden tub in front of a burning hearth. She sighed with pleasure.

"I'll hear that sound again on yer lips soon," Royce called softly.

She couldn't help but giggle. "Aye, you will."

She stripped quickly. Her husband would not be patient about this bath, but she would take what she could.

She contained her moan of pleasure when she sank into the steaming water. She didn't have to force a smile at how good the heat felt. A golden tray held a selection of oils on a small table. She sniffed them one by one: lavender, rose, honey, and something she'd never smelled before. It smelled light, like springtime and sunshine, so she used that, and the scent rose around her with the steam. She leaned against the side of the tub, where a cushion awaited her head, and closed her eyes, relishing the sensual experience—warmth and water and fragrance. Finally, she reached for the selection of soft linen squares and sponges. To get the filth of that hovel where she'd woken that morning off her skin, she chose the coarser sponge.

She took it to the back of her neck, and this time her moan could not be held back. The scrape of the sponge against her filthy skin felt so good.

Royce appeared next to her, and she smiled. She'd known he wouldn't be able to stay away.

"If I hear ye sigh with pleasure one more time, I'll come in my hand."

She burst into gales of laughter and leaned her head back against the soft pillow. "We have all night and every night for forever to lie in each other's arms. Please allow me this wee bit of luxury. There's a sponge under my bottom. It makes it quite comfortable."

"I'll be patient for a bit more. But when ye see me start stripping, ye're in trouble."

"Oh, Royce. I am so utterly happy. I miss my wee lassie so much, but I'm so happy that we will become a family. She needs a good father like you and uncles and aunts. I've kept her hidden too long."

"Ye are a good mother, Rhona. Ye did what ye had to in order to protect her. She is resilient. Ye'll see. She's strong like her mother."

She couldn't help but sigh with pleasure again.

"I'd be pleased to wash ye, love."

"In a few moments." She laid her head back and closed her eyes again, and in momentary stillness, memories of her morning of captivity rushed into her mind. She tried to shake them off as easily as she'd washed away the dirt, but one would not go. "Royce, Father Godfrey told me Ian and Marta are dead."

That caught his attention. "Dead? How? Where? When?"

Rhona shook her head. "He never said for sure. I don't think he knows for sure. Said he heard it near the harbor. He kept insisting he was just trying to save Marta from Ian. He even suggested that Ian killed Marta and then took his own life."

"Hell, could it be true? Do ye believe him, lass?"

"I'm not a lass, Royce."

"Ye were a lass the last time ye were mine alone, so ye still are to me, laaasss." He elongated the word enough to make her roll her eyes.

"I'm not sure what I believe. Tor and Ainsley said they were hale, as far as they could tell. But the entire situation makes me wonder why he would go to such an extent. Why would a priest go all the way to Berwick? And he said he followed Tor and Ainsley back to MacRob land, then followed us. He knew we'd seen the healers. It's possible Ian and Marta left Berwick and were attacked by reivers, but I find that unlikely. If anything happened to them, wouldn't they send word back to MacRob land? Whatever the case, if aught happened to them, it seems Marta's aunt would have sent word back to your clan."

"I agree they would, so we should head home quickly as we can. Mayhap they have heard something by now. Surely the aunt would send word to Marta's family or Marta's father would have found something in his search."

"Agreed. We go home." She handed him the sponge and finally let him have his way. Ah, she'd been waiting for this for so very long. When she'd suggested they marry a sennight ago, she'd told herself it was just to end the feud. She knew now that wasn't her true motivation. She'd wanted him, and ending the feud was merely an added benefit. But . . .

"Speak yer mind. I see that look and I recognize it." He squeezed the sponge and dribbled water over her breasts.

"Why did you turn me down when I first suggested us marrying back in the hunting lodge?" She had to know.

He let out a deep sigh and said, "I was hurt. Even though I knew yer brother forced the wedding with MacAdder, I thought ye might sneak out to see me, let me know ye would miss me or ask for help avoiding the marriage. But I never saw ye again. After all we'd been through, to lose ye so quickly in such a way—it hurt. I never got over ye, Rhona, or we'd no' be here now. But before we met the king and I asked ye about it, ye seemed to have changed yer mind. Why?"

"You had turned me down in the cottage. And I thought you'd forgotten our tree. And . . . and I wanted to marry you for love, not for the feud." She chewed on her bottom lip.

"And ye accused me falsely before the king! Ye're the one who forgot the tree, my daft love. Yer water is cold. How long will ye make me wait to take ye to my bed?"

"It hasn't been that long."

"That quick shot in the lodge doesnae count. I hardly got to hold ye, and ye know that part is special to me." He reached into the water for her ankle, running his finger up her shin to her knee. She stayed completely still while his fingers wandered about her body.

"I think you need to drop that plaid, Laird MacRob."

He stood, dropped it in the blink of an eye, removed his tunic, then sat down on his plaid again. "Now, where was I?"

"At my knee, I believe."

He chuckled, bringing his hand up her thigh, traveling to the vee between her legs. "Will ye let me in yet, lass?"

She shook her head, keeping her eyes closed.

"Hmmm . . . what else do ye like? What can I recall?" His hand moved up to cup her breast, holding the mound in his hand while his thumb teased her nipple.

"Better," she whispered, opening her eyes and repositioning herself in the tub.

"Ye are wiggling. 'Tis a good sign." He used both hands to caress her breasts, teasing her nipples.

She abruptly moved forward, glancing down at his erection. "It still works. You still want me, Royce. I'm so happy to see it."

"Get out and I'll show ye how much I want ye." His voice came out in that husky tone she loved.

"I'll get out, but I wish to dry by the fire. I will not get into that bed all wet."

"I will gladly dry ye, lassie mine."

"You would think we were twenty summers again."

"Ye make me feel twenty summers again." He reached for her hands, and she allowed him to tug her to her feet and help her out of the tub.

"I do not look the same as I did. I'm sorry if I disappoint you."

He took a towel in his hands, faced her toward the hearth, and wrapped the fabric around her. He leaned in to nuzzle her ear. "Ye are still the most beautiful lass in the world to me. And ye look the same. Now hush and allow me to do my work."

"Work?"

"Nay, I misspoke. Ye know I'll enjoy every minute of our time together."

Rhona tried to turn to him, but he stopped her. "No' until ye are completely dry. I do believe yer nipples are quite wet." He brought the towel up and lightly massaged her breasts before moving to her nipples, the edges of the linen oddly exciting. She didn't even try to stop the moan from erupting from her lips, instead leaning back against him.

"You have skilled hands, Royce MacRob."

"For ye, I do, Rhona MacRob."

She smiled at her new name. How wonderful not to be a MacAdder anymore! Her dream had finally come true. She was married to the man she loved, one who adored her.

His hands moved to her bottom as he dried her, caressing her just so.

The man's hands were magical.

She finally could stand it no more and spun around, surprised to see that he'd even lost his hose and stood bare in front of her. "Oh, Royce. You are a fine man."

She wrapped her arms around his neck and kissed him hard on the lips. He scooped her into his arms and carried her to bed.

CHAPTER EIGHTEEN

ROYCE SETTLED HIS lovely wife on the bed, his mouth settling on her knee so he could kiss a trail up her thigh to her core. He sucked her nub until she cried out.

"Stop, please. I need you inside me, Royce."

He grinned and continued his path up her belly, laughing as she gasped, pausing to pay homage to each breast before settling his mouth on hers.

When he ended the kiss, he whispered, "What is that scent ye wear? I dinnae recognize it."

"One of the bottles there. I don't know what it is, but I liked it. Do you?" Her hand traveled down and grasped him, her fingers moving slowly over the velvety skin.

He nuzzled her neck and said, "Aye, I do. Yer skin is still flawless and beautiful. Every bit of ye is soft, I swear it. But ye are bent on torturing me with that hand of yers."

"I can stop anytime."

He leaned back and gazed into her eyes. "Rhona, never stop. I've waited a long time for ye to be mine. I hope I'm no' dreaming."

"Nay, I am yours forever. This should have been ours long ago. Stop teasing—I've waited long enough."

"In time. Dinnae rush me, Rhona. I want to remember our first time as husband and wife." He kissed her cheek while one hand roamed her body, starting at her breasts. He nimbly teased one nipple while he lowered his mouth to her other, circling the taut peak with his tongue. When she cried out, he took the soft mound in his mouth and suckled her, her whimpering driving the hardness in his cock more than anything else could do. "Ye taste better than I recall, sweeting."

His hand moved down to the vee between her legs, parting her curls and teasing her with his finger. All eagerness, she spread her legs for him.

"Your finger is not big enough, Royce. It is not what I need."

He laughed and nuzzled her neck. "I need to make sure ye are ready for me."

"I was ready for you an hour ago, a day ago. I've been thinking of this . . . forever. From the moment ye pinned me to the ground on the obstacle course. Satisfy me, husband," she said, squirming as he pulled his hand away and ran a soft caress over her legs and along her hip. "Do not tease too much or I'll come too quickly. You know I don't like it when that happens."

He could hear the hitch in her breathing, could feel her heartbeat speeding up at his touch so he settled himself over her and teased her entrance with his cock. "This is what ye wish for?"

"Aye, please, Royce. Finish this. You can go slow later."

He could see she was losing patience, so he

thrust inside her until he was fully seated in her heat and her silkiness. She arched beneath him, and her head went back. He held himself still.

"Rhona, look at me, please." His own breathing had become a fast gasping, but he had to say something before he continued. She did, her love evident in her gaze. "Ye are mine forever now. No one will ever hurt ye again. Do ye believe me?"

"Aye. I know you'd never hurt me, Royce."

"Nor will I allow anyone else to hurt ye. No matter what anyone says or does, 'twill no' happen. I searched all of Edinburgh until I found ye, and if I must search all the world to find ye again, I shall do it. Ye are mine forever."

"Aye," she squeaked. She moved against him in a pulsating beat of her pelvis that pushed him too close to the edge. He settled his weight on his elbows and kissed her, finally allowing himself to move, pumping into her until she was nearly at her peak, but he held his own release back. She had to go first.

"Harder, Royce."

He obeyed, then reached between them to touch her in just the right spot. She screamed out his name, the sweetest sound in the world, and he climaxed with her, roaring his satisfaction.

He didn't care who heard them.

As they caught their breath, he stayed on his elbows and set wee kisses on her cheeks and her forehead. He tasted salt. "Ye are crying?"

"Tears of joy. It was so wonderful," she said, trying to slow her breathing. "We are so damn good together. I love you, Royce MacRob."

He grinned. "I love ye, wife. Love the sound of that word also. I'll never tire of hearing ye love me."

Life was great again.

~

They made their way back to MacRob land with mixed emotions, pleased they'd be able to tell everyone there would be no more forced marriages, but saddened by the possibility that Ian and Marta were dead.

"Father Godfrey may well be lying," Royce said. "His behavior in Edinburgh was so daft, can we trust aught he said? I still dinnae understand Ian and Marta's whole story."

"We should keep hoping, but I don't know why he would lie," Rhona said. "We'll say it was what Father Godfrey told us, but it doesn't mean it's true. Mayhap someone else will have seen them."

"I suppose 'tis possible, but it surely puts a damper on our happiness to walk in and say we are married but Marta and Ian are dead." Royce glanced over at Mungo. "Did ye hear or see aught that indicated they're alive or that Godfrey was lying?"

Mungo replied with a shake of his head, "Nay, we asked Odart and Eufemie once Rhona was safe, but they didnae share aught more. I doubt Ian or Marta were ever in Edinburgh if they were seen in Berwick."

When they arrived on MacRob land the second

afternoon of their journey, they were surprised to see so few people about.

Mungo yelled up at the guard at the gate. "Where is everyone?"

"Everyone is moving a bit slow today. Marta and Ian have returned! They arrived midday yesterday, and the celebration went late into the night. But Tor and Ainsley rode with Marta and Ian to Shaw land no' long ago. Did ye no' see them along the way?"

"The two have returned? And hale?" Royce said.

"Aye! Hale and sorry they caused us all such worry. Shall I call a stable lad to grab yer horses?"

"Nay, I expect we'll head to Shaw land." Royce glanced at his wife, who nodded.

"I must see Annie," she replied, "and tell Ainsley our news."

"They left only a wee bit ago," the MacRob guard said. "If ye go now, ye'll no' be far behind them."

"Then we'll head straight there," Royce said. "Mungo, with us. Struan and Tamhas, stay here. One never knows who the true evil ones are sometimes. And tell everyone I finally bring the mistress of MacRob home. Tell my mother we'll be home later tonight."

"She went with Tor," the guard said. "Congratulations to ye, Laird, and to yer new wife."

Royce nodded in acknowledgment. Then they turned their horses toward Castle Shaw.

"I am so happy they have returned," Rhona

said. She looked thoughtful for a long moment. "Royce, don't say anything to Broden about the false betrothal contract yet. I wish to hear about Marta and Ian first, and I don't wish to ruin their return home. I'll speak with my brother privately at another time."

Royce nuzzled her neck quickly, then said, "I agree. We have to announce our marriage, and I dinnae wish to ruin that news either. Ye tell him when ye are ready. I'll leave it to ye."

He was anxious to see everyone, but mostly Marta and Ian. After what Father Godfrey had said, it would be a great relief to see the young pair home and safe.

And he couldn't wait to see if his brother was still madly in love with Ainsley. "Do ye think Tor and Ainsley are still happy?"

"Aye, she adores him, though I cannot believe it. But I am happy for them both."

"We shall see," Royce said with a smirk. It was still hard for him to believe that his brother had fallen hard for that particular woman. Perhaps he had finally matured.

They left their horses in the courtyard of Castle Shaw and hurried to the great hall. What had been raucous conversation rippled into quiet as people noticed them.

It seemed like an opportune moment for Royce to make their announcement. "Greetings to all. I'd like ye to meet my wife, Rhona MacRob."

The group cheered, and Ainsley raced over to her sister to give her a fast hug. "At long last! I'm so happy for ye, Rhona."

Catlin rushed to his side with a fierce hug.

Royce asked, "Ye are still happy, lass?"

"Aye, and I'm even happier now that I know ye will be happy too. Ye belong with her, Royce, but I'm sure ye've known that all along. 'Twas yer stubbornness that kept ye apart."

Royce sighed. "I cannae argue with ye, lass."

Once the congratulatory hugs ended, they made their way over to Ian and Marta, who sat encircled by well-wishers from both clans. They both looked a bit thinner, but Ian's brown eyes were constantly on Marta. He could tell the man was indeed in love, and wondered if he looked the same.

Marta's green eyes were tired, her wavy brown hair plaited, only a few strands escaping. But whenever she looked at her husband, her face lit up.

Perhaps he and Rhona looked the same.

Rhona hugged Ian and said, "We were so worried, especially after we saw Father Godfrey."

Marta took a step back. "Why do ye say that? Ye didnae bring him back with ye, did ye?"

"Nay, I'll have naught to do with him. He's gone mad, I think. He kidnapped me just because we told the king that Tor and Ainsley had seen him in Berwick. He was going to try to force me to say I'd lied about him."

Broden let out a loud whistle to quiet everyone and said, "I think I need to hear the entire story before everyone else does. I'm asking all but my wife, Rhona, Royce, Marta, and Ian to leave."

Ainsley shouted, "And?"

"Fine, ye and Tor may stay also."

"What's wrong?" Marta asked timidly, Ian taking her hand and wrapping his arm around her shoulders.

Royce explained, "We would like to know the entire story. I dinnae know if ye are aware of this, but when the bloody piece of plaid was found and when Marta went missing, our clans turned on each other. MacRobs accused the Shaws of killing ye, Marta."

"King Alexander heard about our troubles and was so incensed that he told us to end the feud or he would start forcing more marriages," Rhona said.

Ian said, "We were told something like that last evening, but 'twas definitely confusing. Is that why ye are all married?"

Broden took his chair and waved everyone closer. "Aye, Catlin and I were the first by the king's decree, but after the moon passed, we were already in love. We were pleased to marry."

Ainsley jumped in to explain their part. "And when King Alexander saw the brawl between the clans that resulted after their marriage, he forced Tor and me to marry. Neither of us were happy about it, but we agreed to go in search of ye two in our quest to end the feud."

Marta's eyes grew huge, then she turned to Royce and Rhona.

Royce said, "No one forced us. I simply married the love of my life." Then he gave Rhona a huge kiss, smacking her lips as loudly as possible. "But we have questions because we heard many conflicting tales of what happened to ye. Ye must share yer story now."

Broden nodded. "Please tell us who was hurt, why ye two were together, and where ye went."

Marta looked to Ian, who said, "I'll explain." He looked from Broden to Royce and took a deep breath. "Marta and I have been sneaking about together, but because of the feud, we didnae wish anyone to know. But I couldnae stand being away from her anymore, so I asked her to marry me. Six moons seemed plenty long to court. We knew we would have to run away, but we thought if we could marry first, it would make the journey easier. Our original plan was to have Father Godfrey marry us, then we would go to her aunt in Berwick and work to earn enough coin to travel to France. Both lairds were sent a missive explaining everything, so why are ye so confused?"

"I received it, but it was confusing, Ian," Broden said. "'Twas so vague it could have meant ye had no intention of hurting Marta. I had no idea it meant ye were married."

"I never received a missive." Royce started pacing. "But clearly things didnae happen the way ye wished, so please explain what actually happened instead of what ye hoped. If Godfrey got his hands on yer message to me, he may have destroyed it."

"Marta spoke with Father Godfrey first," Ian continued. "She asked him if he would meet us in the forest, where we'd no' be seen. We chose the spot, so we went that night and brought a piece of each of our plaids so we would be rightfully handfasted if Father Godfrey didnae come." He squeezed Marta's hand before he continued. "We wouldnae change our minds."

"But I made a mistake and I never realized it until later. I asked Father Godfrey to meet me at the river. I didnae tell him why. I fear he misinterpreted what my intent was." Marta teared up and leaned her head on Ian's shoulder.

Their young love reminded Royce of himself and Rhona as young lovers. They'd sworn nothing could tear them apart. And truly, Ian and Marta had clearly been through a great ordeal, judging by his wary glances and Marta's thin frame. Last he had seen her, she'd been tall but pleasantly soft.

For a while it had seemed like he and Rhona had been wrong about their love, but now, years later, they'd proven they'd been right all along. Their love could not be destroyed. Only their own foolish stubbornness could keep them apart.

He glanced at his wife and saw that her eyes had misted watching the two. He clasped her hand and squeezed it, letting her know the two affected him also.

Ian went on with his story. "When the priest arrived, he had this odd look in his eyes. I recall asking him if he could marry us quickly without a witness. First he said we were too young to marry. I argued and told him he would no' deter us, that Marta and I loved one another, and we would no' be stopped. If he didnae marry us, then we would either handfast or find a priest in Berwick.

"He paced around and around, muttering to himself before he finally stopped. Then he looked at me, and as fast as anyone I've ever seen, he pulled a dagger out of a fold in his robe and came at me. He screamed, 'Marta's mine! If I cannae have her, no one will!' I was so stunned that I didnae know how to reply, especially to a priest. But Marta . . ." Ian paused to kiss her cheek. "Marta tried to intervene, and he cut her leg. I grabbed the weapon so he couldnae do worse. He babbled more about Marta and looked like he wanted to murder me, but he ran off, leaving us to do the best we could."

Broden stood up. "Did ye just tell us that the priest was in love with Marta? And he was the one who wounded her?"

"Aye, strange as it is. He said that although he couldnae marry her, she could be his mistress, that the Church didnae care if a priest took a lover. Said he would return for her. I could have chased him, but I wouldnae leave Marta alone. I cleaned her up the best I could, then placed her on the horse I'd arrived with, and we left."

"Why did ye no' come for help, Ian?" Royce asked.

"We didnae know where Father Godfrey was headed. We didnae wish to see him ever again. And we didnae know if ye would accept our marriage because of the feud. We wouldnae be separated by either of ye or by Father Godfrey. So we started for Berwick and found a healer along the way who stitched Marta's leg. I was glad we found her, because the next day, Marta developed the fever. I didnae know what to do for her, but the healer helped us again."

Royce let go of Rhona's hand. "So Father Godfrey tried to kill ye so he could have Marta to himself? How long has he been watching Marta?"

"We dinnae know," Ian answered. "Marta was as shocked by it as I was."

"Ye could have died without proper care, Marta. What the hell is wrong with Godfrey?" Broden asked. "We thought he was worried about losing his robes, no' that he wished to carry on like a scoundrel. Bloody hell! This makes nae sense to me."

"Do you know that Father Godfrey tried to tell me that he brought Marta to the healer? That he was trying to save Marta from Ian," Rhona declared.

Broden said, "'Tis possible he twisted the entire situation to make himself look like the hero. From what Tor and Ainsley said, he was no' acting right in Berwick either."

Marta whispered, "The man made no sense. He is a priest who didnae act like one. He followed us to Berwick and chased us there. We didnae know if he wished to steal me away or kill Ian, or some other evil plan. We hid everywhere we could."

"Tor and Ainsley decided to head to Berwick to find ye, along with several patrols in search of ye all the time," Broden said. "I know no' how ye evaded all the guards we had looking for ye."

"We saw ye. I called out to ye, but then ye went the other way. Why?" Tor asked.

"Because I saw Father Godfrey no' far from ye. He frightened me and he looked as though he was half crazed by then. I thought the man would never leave us alone," Marta said. "Bishop Timlin found out Father Godfrey was in Berwick, where he had no business being, and then he disappeared. My aunt said the bishop sent men out to bring him back but they couldnae locate him anywhere, so we decided he returned here because he never caught up with us. Aunt Mary's priest married us, and we decided to come home so as no' to cause any trouble for my aunt. We thought it safest to be with our clans, and it would take years and years to save enough coin to get to France."

Royce stood up to tell his part. "We found Father Godfrey—or I should say he found us— in Edinburgh. Rhona and I spoke with the king about the feud, and the king graciously allowed us to spend the night in the castle. Godfrey paid coin to the healers and another man to help him kidnap Rhona. Still dinnae know how he did it, but I saw the healers and they admitted to helping him, though they knew no' why he was paying them to distract the guards. He abducted Rhona and held her in a hut outside the burgh."

Rhona cut in. "The strangest part was Father Godfrey. He told me Ian tried to kill you, Marta, and that he was trying to save you. He couldn't find you in Berwick, so he followed Tor and Ainsley home and then followed Royce and me to Edinburgh, because he thought maybe we knew where you were. He even followed us into the castle and heard what we told the king.

That's why he stole me away. He wanted me to convince the king that he was trying to save Marta and that he'd done nothing wrong. I think he was seriously afraid he would be defrocked."

Ian said, "And do no' forget he still wished for Marta to be his mistress. He wanted to come out without any problems and come back here to live as the priest with Marta as his mistress."

Broden said, bolting to his feet, "Bloody hell. That man is nae priest. Why would he kidnap ye? I still am no' sure I believe that our priest caused so many problems. He surely has lost his mind, and I know not how to handle it if he returns."

Rhona shuddered, and Royce knew exactly why. He felt the same chill at the priest's actions. He laid his hand on her shoulder as she answered. "I doubt he will dare return here after all that has transpired. The healers suggested he might be involved with Ian and Marta's disappearance, but we couldn't see the truth in it. We left him in Edinburgh after revealing all, so King Alexander was going to speak with the bishop about sanctioning him. Not allowing him back here until he served his punishment, though we know not what that was to be."

"I still cannae believe a priest abducted ye from the king's castle. Where were the castle guards?" Tor asked.

Rhona glared at Tor. "He used his collar and trickery, hoping to force me to recant my story about him being seen in Berwick. He said once I recanted, he'd set me free. He spent much time trying to convince everyone that he was trying to save Marta, that it was the only reason he left the Highlands. His purpose was commendable, but I don't think anyone believed him, especially after he kidnapped me." Then she looked up at Royce and smiled. "Father Godfrey never made it to the king with me. Royce and his men rescued me." She grinned and gave Royce's hand a quick kiss. "And I'll also mention that Father Godfrey tried to tell me you were both dead at one point."

"Both of us? How?" Ian asked. "And why would he tell such a lie?"

Rhona glanced at Royce, then said, "He never said how, but I think he was trying to make us believe you and Marta were dead so we would stop looking for you."

Royce added, "If we'd found Marta and Ian, they'd have told the truth about all that happened at the river, and he didnae want the king hearing that he'd stabbed Marta. He'd have been defrocked quickly."

"So is Father Godfrey still alive or did ye kill a priest, MacRob?" Broden asked.

"Nay, I couldnae kill him, but I did give him my fist. And he is with the king, who will decide his punishment for kidnapping Rhona. And he'll have to answer to the bishop."

"I'm glad to hear it. He deserved more than a fist, I think," Broden said. "Well, I'm pleased we are all home and happy. Marta and Ian, ye are welcome to stay on Shaw soil."

"Or MacRob soil," Tor shouted.

"We'll let them choose."

Marta and Ian rose. Marta gave Royce and

Broden a tired curtsy. "If ye'll excuse us, I'd like to go see my parents. I miss my sister."

"And my mother also," Ian added.

Rhona stood as well. "I must go find my daughter and Forsy. Is she abovestairs, Ainsley?"

"They are well. I took good care of my new niece," Broden said, a little defensively Royce thought. "They are in the keep."

Catlin added, "She is the sweetest thing, Rhona."

Rhona nodded, then looked to Royce. "Are ye ready?"

The four newlyweds left the hall while the others remained behind.

"The two of you must be exhausted," Rhona said. "Marta, does your leg still pain you?"

"Nay, no' so much now. But I surely am weary. And ye must be also."

"I am. I'll see my lassie and then find a place for a nap. We'll walk with you to the stables. It's a lovely night," Rhona said, leaning against her husband.

Ian and Marta collected their horses and were readying to mount up when a rustling noise came from the forest next to them. Marta caught her breath and spun to look.

"'Tis probably a deer foraging for food," Royce said, paying little mind to the sound.

Marta shrieked and ducked behind Ian.

A man in priest's robes stepped from the trees carrying a sword at his side. "Marta, finally I have found ye."

Royce's sword was in his hand without thought,

and he pushed Rhona behind him.

"Ian, he's coming for ye!" He shouted the warning, but Ian stood steady and pulled out his dagger.

"I'll no' hurt ye, Ian, but Marta loves me. Ye can forget all that happened and just allow us to spend time together. Marta, is that no' what ye wish?" Father Godfrey looked like a different man, gaunt and wild-eyed, though his gaze did carry a bit of adoration whenever he looked at Marta. "I'm sure we can work this out, Ian. Twice a sennight 'tis all I ask for. She has enough love in her heart for two men, Ian. Ye can have bairns with her, just share her for a short time. I promise to treat her well."

"Nay, I love Ian and only Ian, Father. Please leave us be." Marta stood firmly behind her husband.

"How the hell did ye get away from the king's men?" Royce asked, his sword ready to strike at the man.

"The bishop believed me. He knew in my heart that everything I did was to help save Marta from Ian. I have some minor sanctions, but that is all. Do ye all forget I am a man of God? I am trying to do God's work here."

"A man of God does no' kidnap a woman for his own use," Royce bellowed. "Or have ye forgotten that? Does a man of God tell someone that two people are dead when they are no'? I will make sure to remind the bishop when I see him next. Or mayhap I'll pen him a missive about yer behavior."

"I said they were dead so ye would stop looking for them. Ye were in my way. Ye'll no' have the chance to pen that missive, MacRob!" The look in the priest's eyes changed, the fury now there enough for Royce to grip his weapon tighter.

"I hate ye all! Everyone but my sweet Marta." Godfrey ran at Ian, but Royce moved too quickly, cutting off his path. Royce's sword bit into the madman's arm, causing him to drop his sword and scream in pain.

Godfrey's face twisted into a snarl. His hair was wild and his eyes wide and unblinking. "Then I'll take Rhona as my mistress." He moved toward her, his biggest mistake.

"Ye'll never touch her." Royce lunged, and his sword caught the troubled priest in his belly.

Rhona screamed and hid her face. Marta and Ian backed away from the dying man, catching at the panicked horses' reins.

Broden and Tor sprinted out of the great hall, their swords drawn, and Mungo ran toward them from the stable.

Father Godfrey crumpled to the ground before any of them arrived.

He'd bother Marta no more.

CHAPTER NINETEEN

THEY DINED AT Castle Shaw that eve, since Ian and Marta had been celebrated by the MacRobs the night before. It seemed to Rhona that Annie had grown a hand taller in the five days she'd been away. The lass had babbled on and on about all her new friends and how she loved the castle.

Rhona guessed her wee lassie would adjust just as easily to her new home in Castle MacRob. She smiled as she watched Annie, growing up so quickly, playing with Eby near the hearth.

Rhona turned to Royce and couldn't resist pushing a stray lock of hair out of his eyes. "Are you happy, husband?"

"I am. I dinnae need to worry about a daft priest coming for ye any longer. And I'll have ye with me in Castle MacRob, and yer daughter too, and Forsy if she'd like, and become the family we should have been long ago."

"I'm anxious to see your chamber, my lord. Will you allow me to add a few of my things?"

"Add whatever ye like. 'Tis yer chamber also. Ye'll no' sleep in a separate bed, no' in my castle."

She kissed him and said, "I wouldn't dream of

sleeping anywhere but in your arms."

The meal passed with a strange mix of joy and sorrow. Reunion and tragedy made for strange companions at the table. Clan members finished their meal and headed to their homes. The guards ate and resumed their posts or went to their beds. This meal, unlike the one the night before, would not go long into the night, fueled by toasts and laughter.

Eventually, only Broden and Catlin remained, sitting on the dais with Royce and Rhona. Ainsley and Tor had left to put Annie to bed.

Catlin said, "So the most wonderful news of this, besides seeing Ian and Marta both hale and happy, is that the famous feud between the MacRobs and the Shaws is finally over. After twelve years, 'tis done."

Rhona felt her stomach twist and looked to Royce for his reaction, but he said nothing, instead reaching for her hand under the table. While it might be true that the rest of the clan members felt no more animosity between them, she could not feel at peace.

"Nay, not for me."

Her brother, looking as much like a laird as she'd ever seen him, leaned back and said, "Exactly what do ye mean by that statement, sister?"

Rhona had thought hard about what she should say to her brother, whether she should even try to make him understand, but she was still angry about what he'd done, how his actions had torn her life apart, so nearly beyond repair. She'd talked with Broden and been civil, but it was time to let him know what they'd learned from the king.

Royce, who always understood her so well, gave her a brief nod of encouragement.

She pushed her chair back and stood up. "I'll not make peace with you until I understand how you could have thought that betrothal agreement was genuine. You knew Da thought highly of Royce." She stopped, gathering her thoughts before continuing. "Broden, Duncan MacAdder forged those signatures on the betrothal agreement. The king never signed any contract, said he wouldn't have agreed to it. Da never agreed to any betrothal. You should have known he never would."

Catlin's eyes widened as she peered at Rhona, then she turned to her husband, demurely folding her hands on her lap.

Broden gave his wife's cheek a quick kiss and stood up. "Rhona, I've apologized to ye already. When will ye let this go, or do ye just prefer to keep it going forever? What is yer problem?"

"My problem is what we learned from King Alexander was so shocking that I did not wish to bring it up during the festival, but I cannot hold my tongue any longer. Did you hear what I said, Broden?"

Broden smirked and lifted his palm as encouragement. "I heard you, but since I saw the agreement, I know no' of what ye speak. But if ye must go on and on, then please do. Go ahead, Rhona. Please attack me again if 'twill ease yer pain."

"Dinnae act like that with me, brother." Rhona

was ready to spit at him, though surprised to hear herself slip back into her Scottish brogue.

Royce placed his hand on her arm and stood next to her. "King Alexander said there was nae such agreement between yer sire and MacAdder."

Broden paused momentarily, as if the meaning of their words were just finally sinking in. "What are ye talkin' about? I saw the agreement. I saw Da's signature and the king's."

"Da never signed it, Broden. King Alexander said he never would have approved a marriage between me and Duncan. He knew of the relationship between Royce and me, and the king said he was more surprised than anyone to hear I wed another. That document was false, Broden. False!"

Royce's mother, Helen, stepped into the hall, finding a seat nearby, but she said nothing.

Broden sat down, his gaze locked on his sister. "Rhona, I saw it with my own eyes. It promised a betrothal to one of my sisters."

Rhona shook her head, her whole body trembling from what she'd suffered because of that document—a creation of Duncan MacAdder. "After I had Annie and while he was beating me, he said something, and I did not recall it until King Alexander spoke. Duncan told me he was sorry he ever made everything up, that I was not worth it. I didn't know what he meant, but now I do."

She fell back into her own seat, her mind tracing through many different conversations, thoughts of how young her brother had been back then, not even twenty, how naïve.

"Ye should have verified it with the king, Shaw," Royce said. "Rhona was to be my wife, though it was no' made formal. Because ye accepted MacAdder's betrothal agreement and I didnae marry, I disappointed my sire and may have had a part in his death."

Helen stood up quickly and said, "Dinnae say that again, Royce. 'Tis no' true."

Rhona couldn't stop, could not hold her tongue. "If we had married, everything would have been different. Our lives could have been happy. Why didn't you try to help me, Broden?"

"Why did ye no' stand up to the mean bastard? Ye knew he was no' right in his mind," Royce said.

"Nay, I didnae. How would I have known he was daft? He was laird of his clan. I did what I could by protecting Ainsley."

"But ye could have done more. Ye did naught, Shaw!" Royce bellowed.

"And after the wedding, you abandoned me." Rhona could not stop the flood of pain and grief she'd stored up over the years. Tears of anger, sorrow, and hurt streamed down her cheeks, and she let them fall. "Why could you not have checked on me after everything that happened? You left me there. He wouldn't allow me out, and you never came to see how I fared."

"Bloody hell, Rhona, but I did!" Broden bellowed, bolting out of his chair. "I tried many times, but I was told ye refused me, that ye were too angry with me to ever speak to me again.

Can ye no' see how I would believe that?"

"But after Annie was born. After I was beaten . . ."

"I helped ye the only way I thought ye'd allow. Who do ye think arranged for yer cottage? Provided yer food and comfort. I heard what he'd done to ye and told Giric to prepare the cottage. Had him supply ye with wood and food and all else ye might have needed. I didnae desert ye."

Royce slammed his fist on the table. "But ye didnae seek satisfaction. I did. With every fist to his mouth, I told him he was never to touch Rhona again. Ye are her brother. Why did ye no' step forward?"

"I did. I took Giric one night and we tracked him down. He'd already suffered one beating, which I suppose now must have been ye, and I warned him to stay away. I told him if he ever came near that cottage or set foot on our land, I'd kill him with my bare hands. I made sure he'd never touch ye again. Rhona, ye must believe me. I did no' desert ye."

Rhona was in shock, looking from Royce to her brother. "You did that for me? I thought it was Giric."

"Giric works for me, or have ye forgotten?"

"Oh, Broden. I had no idea."

Broden moved closer. "I've apologized to ye for allowing the marriage. I knew naught about the falsification. The signature looked like Da's, and how would I have known what King Alexander's signature looked like? If it was forged, someone did a fine job. I was young and naïve. MacAdder was forceful. I thought I had nae choice but to honor an agreement made by our father. But dinnae forget, Rhona. Ye are the one who wished to go in Ainsley's place. If I'd betrothed Ainsley to him, that could have given us the time to uncover his lies, since she was too young to marry."

"Nay, he wished to marry Ainsley right away," Rhona said. "I couldnae allow that."

"What did ye say?" Ainsley and Tor had returned without Rhona noticing. Ainsley moved closer to her brother. "Please repeat what ye just said. I was supposed to marry MacAdder instead of Rhona?"

Rhona took one look at Ainsley and felt weighted down with all that had happened, all the wrong paths and missed turnings, all the decisions made wrongly or not made at all. She had never wished to hurt her dear sister, indeed had made all her decisions to protect her. Now she stood in front of the sister she loved more than anything, happily married yet suddenly weary and sad. She didn't know if she could fix this, but she had to try.

But the hot tempers in the hall finally blew.

Tor stepped forward until he was nose-to-nose with Broden. "Ye wished to marry my wife to the bastard MacAdder? How old was she? He would have killed her. Broden, ye would have sent a lass to be tortured just to meet MacAdder's wishes?"

"Stand back, Tor. We thought if we told him Rhona was already spoken for, he would forget the agreement, but then he decided he wanted Ainsley. We said she was too young. And ye didnae care about her at all back then, so dinnae pretend ye would have been mortally wounded by the match."

Broden shoved Tor's shoulder, and the younger man took a single step back, stared at Broden for a long, angry moment, then started pacing. He fixed his gaze on his own brother then.

"Royce, ye would have allowed Ainsley to marry the devil to preserve yer marriage?"

Royce shook his head, seemingly as much from regret as denial. "I knew naught about that. I was never consulted. Mayhap I should have come and spoken to Broden, but I was a fool in love, much hurt by the decision. I knew naught of MacAdder's wish to marry Ainsley. Knew little of the document. I was in love with Rhona and would have done aught to marry her. She was to be my wife, have my bairns, give me heirs, but instead there are none and I disappointed my sire."

"I knew what I was doing, Tor," Rhona admitted. "I wished to protect Ainsley. If it had to be one of us, I knew it had to be me. I love you too much, Ainsley, to have sent you to that evil man. But that doesn't change the fact that it *didn't* have to be *either* of us."

Ainsley fell into a chair, tears on her cheeks.

"Now look what ye've both done to my sister," Broden said. "Yer insistence on keeping the past alive is still causing pain. Ye've upset her when she didnae need to know any of this."

Royce moved closer to Broden, his finger pointed in accusation. "If ye'd done what any laird would have done, this wouldnae have happened."

"If ye were so damn wise, why did ye no' suggest it to me, MacRob? Ye think ye were so wise, but were ye in the same place I was, ye'd have done the same thing. Ye are going to tell me if someone handed ye a document today with yer sire's signature on it, one that looked exactly like his signature, ye would no' honor it? If ye try to tell me so, ye are a liar."

Rhona held her arms up to call for silence. To her surprise, they all stopped talking and stared at her. She paused for a moment to collect her thoughts, then said, "Ainsley, there was no way I would have allowed you to be married to the man. I did not like the way he looked at me, as if he were always undressing me, but the looks he gave you were far worse. The fault is Broden's. He should have known our father would never make such an agreement. He should have checked the document."

"How the hell was I to check a document? Ye presume too much. Why will ye no' let this go, Rhona? 'Tis time, sister. Time to let it all be in our past, never to be mentioned again. We all made mistakes, and they cannae be undone."

Rhona's face burned with fury. "Because it didn't ruin your life! It ruined mine. If you had stood up against that evil man, everything would have been different. Everything!"

"Mama?" A small figure walked quietly into the middle of the hall and stood directly in front of her mother. Silence fell, everyone holding their breath.

Rhona had no idea how much her wee lassie had heard. But she learned quickly.

"Mama, do you wish I was different too?"

"Och, nay!" Rhona let out a wee sob and reached for her daughter. "Nay, I'm so sorry, sweeting. I'd never change anything about you." She hugged Annie tight and breathed in the scent of her daughter's hair, and fought to control her emotions so her child wouldn't see her cry. "I didn't mean it. Truly I did not. And I will fix this now."

She stood tall and took Annie's hand in hers. All the hall was quiet, Ainsley wiping her tears, Catlin still as a statue, the men as tense as if they were going into battle. Rhona and Annie moved over to her brother.

"Broden, I apologize to you. You were young and you made the best decision you could." She stopped to gaze down at her daughter, the full realization of what she'd nearly done falling upon her shoulders. Her foolish temper had betrayed her again.

If she could unwind time, losing both Annie and the torture, would she do it?

Never. Annie was worth every bit of suffering, and she'd do it again just to have the delight of her dear daughter.

"I love you, Broden, and I hope we can get to know each other again. Though the years have been hard, your decision gave me my greatest gift, my sweet Annie." She nearly choked on tears over that last sentence.

Royce came over behind Rhona, leaned down

to kiss Annie's head, and said to Broden, "Since we are already married, I didnae have the chance to ask for yer blessing, but I ask ye for it now. I promise to treat Rhona well and protect her with my life."

Broden nodded. "It should have happened long ago. Had I known the truth, I would have approved yer marriage."

Then Royce knelt in front of Annie. "Lass, since ye are the most important person in yer mother's life, the one she loves more than aught, I wish to ask if ye will accept me as yer mother's husband. That means I will love her and protect her for all of my days, and the two of ye will come and live with me in my castle. And if ye agree, I'd like to be yer father, act as if ye are mine alone. I promise ye both will be precious to me."

Annie looked up at her mother, who had new tears—happy tears—falling now, then looked at the other faces in the hall. Tor, Ainsley, Catlin, Broden, and Helen.

"I agree only if you all stop fighting. You yell too loud. I was asleep in the other chamber."

The group laughed and agreed.

Royce held his hand to his heart and said, "I pledge never to yell at yer mama. Nor Uncle Broden, Aunt Catlin, or yer aunt Ainsley. But I'm no' sure if I can promise never to yell at Uncle Tor. He likes to anger me whene'er he can. I think ye'll believe me that I'll no' yell at my own mother."

Helen said, "She'll yell at ye if ye dinnae stop blaming yer father's death on yer own decisions.

He had a bad heart for a long time."

Royce looked at his mother and nodded. Rhona hadn't realized he'd carried such a weighty burden, but he seemed to lay it down now, accepting the truth of his mother's words. "I promise, Mama."

Rhona moved closer to peer down at her daughter. "Do you accept him, Annie? Do you think he'll make a good father?"

Annie nodded.

"Thank ye, Annie lass." Royce kissed her hand, then kissed Rhona on the lips. She let herself step into his open arms, and he lifted her off her feet to hug her.

Annie said, "Please, may I be excused?"

Rhona gave her an odd look.

Annie gave a long-suffering sigh and said, "I'm tired and you're kissing again."

CHAPTER TWENTY

RHONA STRETCHED AND finally got out of the bed she shared with Royce. He'd been up for ages, gone early for a hunting trip. She washed her face and tidied her plait, then pulled on a simple gown and padded down the stairs to the great hall. Annie and Helen sat at one of the tables talking and giggling, and Rhona smiled at the perfect scene in front of her.

Her sennight as Royce's wife had been wonderful. Annie had adjusted easily and made new friends. Aunt Ainsley had begun teaching Annie to read. And Rhona herself had taken up some of Helen's duties as the new mistress of the castle. The older woman had been nothing but welcoming and patient with her new daughter-in-law.

But the best part was lying in Royce's arms every night. She adored him more each day.

She stepped over to the table and leaned down to speak with Annie. "Greetings, my sweet. What are you eating this morn?"

"Greetings, Mama. We have porridge with honey and berries. Grandmama taught me how to sweeten my porridge. I like honey in my porridge."

"Ooh, berries are my favorite," Rhona said, kissing her daughter on the top of her head. "Did you sleep well?"

"Aye. Eby's stuffed puppy is my favorite. He sleeps with me. And I have a new friend Izzy here who is five summers just like me. And Grandmama read me a wonderful story last eve. Mama, I like having a grandmama."

"I do too, lassie. She's one of the things that makes me so happy to be here. Grandmama is a wise woman, and I have much to learn. And I love that you have two new friends, Eby at Castle Shaw and Izzy is here." She squeezed Helen's hand and said, "Do you know when Royce will be back from his hunting trip? I was surprised when he told me about it, since they just returned from a long trip the other day."

"He didnae tell me. He, Tor, and Mungo all went today. Normally, one of those three stays here when the other two are away. But I didnae ask about it."

Ainsley came down the stairs yawning.

"Someone was up a bit late last eve?" Rhona teased.

Ainsley gave a contented sigh and said, "Aye." Then she blushed and peeked over at Helen. "Forgive me, Helen."

Helen barked out a laugh. "I couldnae be happier to hear ye talk like that. Means more grandbairns for me. The question is who will be first?" She ruffled the top of Annie's hair. "Would ye like a little brother or sister, Annie lass?"

The door banged open, and Struan came in. "Someone at the gates to see ye, mistress."

He scowled more fiercely than Rhona had ever seen.

She narrowed her gaze. "Who? I don't like the look on your face, Struan."

"MacAdders," Struan spat. "Duncan's brother Malcolm and his second-in-command, Simon."

"Well, I'd be happy to see those two piles of dung. Helen, please take Annie over to the keep. Bring Izzy along and they can play there this morn. I'm sure her mother won't mind."

Helen and Annie hurried to the kitchens to find Izzy. Ainsley said, "Are ye sure ye wish to receive him, Rhona? I dinnae think ye should allow him in while Royce and Tor are gone."

"Nay, I'll see him outside. He doesn't deserve to set foot in Castle MacRob proper. Struan, tell them to wait outside. I'll come out in a moment, and tell the rest of the guards to be alert. I'll have you stand at my back while I'm speaking with them."

"Aye, my lady. I'll no' leave yer side." He strode out the door ahead of her.

Rhona took her time in the hall, taking an oatcake and some berries from the sideboard for her breakfast. She washed the food down with a few swallows of cider.

Ainsley followed her example and got her own breakfast. "What was his brother like?" she asked.

Rhona swallowed her bite of fruit—oh, they were extra good this year, sweet and soft. Or maybe they were reflecting the turn of her life.

"He's a spineless bastard. When Duncan beat me for birthing a lass instead of a lad, he ordered Malcolm and Simon to hold me. Malcolm did his share of beating. He pinched my nipple, stomped on my breast. And when I bit him, he punched me in my female parts. It hurt so bad because I'd just given birth, I thought I was going to pass out. And Simon followed right along."

Ainsley's eyes narrowed in a familiar way— Rhona had learned to look out when her sister looked at her that way, and she almost smiled at the thought of her sister's wrath unleashed on Malcolm and Simon.

"Let's go see the fools," Ainsley said. "Ye're no' scared?"

Rhona shook her head. "Nay. I'm ready to see them. No reason to hold off dealing with the scum any longer."

She didn't delay because she was afraid, but because she owed these men nothing. She made them wait because she *could*. Here at Castle MacRob, she had the power. Finally, she brushed invisible crumbs from her skirts, grabbed her mantle, and went out, Ainsley at her side.

"Be careful, Ainsley. Hold your temper. I don't want you hurt." She moved ahead of her sister and stepped to the gates, motioning for Struan to open them. A little cluster of men on horseback awaited her, Malcolm and Simon in front and ten guards arrayed behind them. The spineless fools hadn't even gotten off their horses. Perhaps they truly were cowards and wanted to be able to make a quick retreat. "What do you want, MacAdder?"

"I'd like to speak privately with you in your hall, my lady."

"My lady. Well, isn't that a wee bit out of character for you, Malcolm? You are not welcome in my hall, but if you wish to speak to me, get off your horse."

Malcolm smirked but hid it quickly, and she could see the deceit in his eyes. What could he possibly want?

He dismounted and nodded to Simon, who followed suit. When they approached her, she found herself suddenly flanked by more than a dozen MacRob guards, all with their hands on the hilt of their swords. She could tell from the sound of rattling shafts that the archers on the curtain wall pulled arrows from their quivers.

Aye, she was now mistress of the castle, and these guards would protect her. Malcolm's men could not hold up long against these MacRobs.

"What do you want, Malcolm? Be quick about it." She crossed her arms and waited to hear what his purpose was.

"I brought a decree with me to read to you."

"Leave it. I'll read it myself in my own time."

"You needn't read it. I'll tell you. This is signed by King Alexander. Now that my brother is dead, he has approved our marriage after giving you sufficient time to grieve."

"Our marriage?" She glanced at her sister in surprise. "Does this daft man mean he wishes to marry me?"

"I think so. Apparently, he doesnae know ye are already married to Royce MacRob." Ainsley crossed her arms and smiled. "So ye may all take yer leave. Ye've wasted yer time coming here."

"I assure you our time is not wasted. The order includes an annulment of your marriage to MacRob because I have the right to marry one of the Shaw sisters first. I choose you, Rhona. You were such a fine wife to my brother, and it is important to keep our lineage the same. You must bring my niece with you. I wish to get to know her."

Rhona began to laugh, slapped her thigh once, then looked at her sister and laughed harder.

"Laugh all you wish, but if you do not come willingly, the sheriff will arrest you. The writ declares it to be so by the pen of King Alexander."

"May I see it, please?" Rhona asked.

Malcolm handed it over to Rhona. She looked at it, showed it to her sister, and then she threw it on the ground and stepped on it, using her heel to grind it deeply into the ground.

Malcolm smirked again. "We expected that response, so we have two copies. You have until sundown on the morrow. If you do not come to MacAdder Castle, I will send the sheriff for you."

This time he gave her a huge smile and waggled his brow at her.

Rhona spat at him.

He and Simon mounted their horses, and their company rode away.

"We'll be back on the morrow with the sheriff!" Simon called over his shoulder.

Though Struan dismissed the guard, many of the men stayed near and took up posts outside the castle wall.

"My lady, could it be true?" Struan asked.

"Nay." She turned on her heel and marched back into the hall.

Ainsley followed, peppering her with questions. "Was it real, Rhona? Could he really do that? Do ye think the sheriff will arrest ye and annul yer marriage? Royce will kill him. I wish we knew where they were. Would the king sign something like that?"

"Nay! I know for certain he would not. 'Tis another false document, Ainsley. Count on it." Rhona was nearly out of her mind with outrage. The same trick! They weren't even smart enough to come up with some other ruse. "We just saw the king, sister. He was at our wedding. Malcolm is lying."

"I ought to have dumped my chamber pot over his head," Ainsley said. "Sit down and I'll find ye a goblet of wine."

"Nay, I wish to think clearly." She took a chair in front of the hearth. "We must prepare in case he does return, but Royce and Tor will know best what to do."

"The only part I worry about is the sheriff. He might be taken in by the false document and attempt to enforce it." Ainsley reached for her sister's hand. "But Royce will never allow it. Ye know he'll protect ye from whoever comes."

"I know." And she did know. Royce had promised to protect her, and she trusted him more than any other in the world. She just wished he were here. She stood up again and began to brush off her shoulders and her arms, everywhere. "Malcolm makes me feel so dirty. I need a bath."

Rhona paced, Ainsley sitting there with her and trying to distract her, but it was no good. All she could think of was that fool's face when he'd stomped on her. How dare he come here now?

It seemed like hours passed. No one came into the hall, and once or twice Rhona caught sight of Forsy turning people away.

No matter how much she paced, how much she thought, she couldn't completely banish her worry. She *knew* the king had signed no such order. She *knew* Royce would protect her. She *knew* Malcolm could not force her to marry him. But he apparently still had power over her—he could still throw her mind into turmoil.

Ainsley at one point said, "Rhona, Royce adores ye. He'll never let ye go. Sit down or ye'll exhaust yerself. They'll be home soon, and then we can make plans."

Soon didn't come for hours.

A long time later, the door opened, and Royce came in, Tor right behind him. "Rhona? Ye look distressed, my lass. Did something happen while we were away?"

"Oh, Royce," she sighed. She hugged him hard, grateful for his solidity. She stood back and looked into his worried eyes. "You won't believe who was here this morn. Malcolm MacAdder came here with Simon and some of their guards. He had another false document, and he tried to tell me the king has ordered the annulment of our marriage so I can marry Malcolm. He's threatening to send the sheriff for Annie and me on the morrow." Angry, anxious tears gathered, and she wanted to stomp her foot like a wee lass.

Tor put his arm around Ainsley, who said, "Tor, we must do something."

Tor shook his head and said, "Royce will handle it."

Rhona leaned her head on Royce's shoulder and stopped her tears. She had to focus and help her husband put a stop to Malcolm's scheme. They would stay together this time, no matter what any MacAdder might try.

"Royce, we must prepare. We all know his document is forged, just like the first, but the sheriff might not be able to see through this charade. I would rather go to jail than let Malcolm touch me, but I'd rather not do that either." Her mind drifted back to those nasty times, and she gave a little shudder.

Royce lifted her chin to face him. Then he put his finger up to her lips and said, "Aye, love, ye know I'll no' let aught happen to ye. But even jail wouldnae separate us. I'd just go along with ye, and we'd make so much noise, the sheriff would kick us out."

Rhona couldn't contain a little laugh. "I'd almost like to try it. But where have you been? Are your hunting trips usually so long?" She caught sight of his hand, his knuckles split and swollen in one spot. She cradled it in her own two hands. "What happened to your hand?"

"Our prey was elusive today, but we hunted 'em down. Is that no' right, Tor?"

"Aye, we had a wonderful time too," Tor said, smiling at Ainsley. Rhona swore he winked at his wife.

"In fact, we brought the beasts back alive," Royce said. "Ye should come out and see them. Stay with me and do as I say, and they'll no' hurt ye."

Rhona took a step back from him and the door. "What were you thinking, Royce? Did you catch a wolf and bring it home as a pet? You should have taken it to MacAdder Castle and locked it in."

Tor gave a little snort of laughter.

Royce reached for her hand and tugged her forward again, just a light tug, and she allowed it. "Aye, two wolves, of a sort. But they'll no' be anyone's pets. Come and see, and ye'll understand."

The door flew open, and her brother stood there. "What the bloody hell is taking so long?"

"Broden?" Seeing her brother in the MacRob hall was so odd that she just stood and blinked at him for a moment. "Why are you here?"

"Rhona, listen to Royce. Ye need to come outside." He stepped aside and gestured for them to go into the courtyard.

She couldn't understand what was happening, and she was getting tired of all these men trying to boss her around. None of them seemed to understand the situation. "Broden, Malcolm MacAdder was here. He's trying Duncan's trick and waving around a false document that says I have to marry him."

Broden rolled his eyes. "Rhona, we will no' let

that happen to ye again." He used that voice, the one he used to calm people down, which he was so good at. It was part of why he was a good laird, despite his difficult start as the head of the clan.

"But we should be ready, in case they return with the sheriff. And the king should be notified that his signature has been forged. Surely 'tis treason!" Then she caught sight of her brother's hands, which looked much like Royce's—split skin and bruised knuckles. "Broden, were you hunting with Royce?"

He grinned. "Aye, exactly. We were hunting. Royce and Tor and I all went hunting. They stopped when they passed through Shaw land and asked me if I wished to go with them."

"Your hands look worse than Tor's or Royce's." She whirled to face Tor. "Mayhap *you'll* tell me what's going on." But the younger man just grinned and shook his head, pursing his lips the odd way he often did.

Royce looked at Broden over her head and said, "Are they ready?"

"Aye, everything is ready for ye."

"Rhona, I sense ye're ready to storm MacAdder's castle or boil some oil in case of attack. But ye might change yer plans after ye step outside. Trust me and yer brother, though I know 'tis hard. Come outside."

She stared into his eyes, the love she saw in his gaze overpowering her, making her believe that he would take care of her. No matter what happened, they would face it together.

Broden said, "Rhona, trust yer husband."

She looked at her brother and she swore he had tears in his eyes, but she had to be mistaken.

She rolled her eyes. "Fine. Let's get this over with."

She'd admire the lads' catch and then they could boil the oil.

She stepped out through the door, Royce on one side, Broden on the other, Ainsley and Tor right behind them. She was surprised to see so many MacRobs in the courtyard.

All staring at her.

But not just blue plaids. The green Shaw plaids were here too. They mingled, men and women, blue and green, side by side, all waiting solemnly, as if for a sacred rite.

"Royce, what is this?"

"I had a particular quarry in mind for this hunting trip, and yer brother was eager to join me. I've been planning it since we returned from Edinburgh, but I had nae idea I would pick the perfect day for it." He led her down the steps, her brother on the other side of her.

Not so long ago, she'd hated the two men who now stood on either side of her. Now she loved them so much it pained her.

They escorted her to the center of the courtyard, all her clanmates watching. A dozen men in the king's livery stood at attention opposite the crowd. What?

Then she understood.

Royce turned her toward the royal guard, and she froze. Two men were there, stripped of their plaids and tunics, their arms chained and fastened over their heads to a post. Their faces were bruised and bloody, and splotches of purple and blue blossomed across their torsos.

Malcolm and Simon.

She shook her head, not wanting them here. Not wanting anything to do with them.

Royce said, "Will the king's captain join us, please?"

One of the guards, garbed in chain mail and a tunic bearing King Alexander's red lion, joined them.

"By word of King Alexander, do ye grant this woman the right of due justice for these men's crimes committed upon her?" Royce spoke loud enough for all to hear him.

"Aye, we are here to serve justice upon these men for the lies of their clan and the harm inflicted upon Rhona Shaw MacRob. When local justice has been served, we will take custody and remove them to Edinburgh to face the king's justice. King Alexander has confirmed Duncan MacAdder's only child, Annie MacAdder MacRob, as heir to the MacAdder lairdship, along with all rights, responsibilities, and property thereof. Rhona Shaw MacRob will designate a steward and caretaker until the child comes of age."

Rhona stared at the captain, her mind churning in turmoil. Of course Annie would be Duncan's heir, since she was his child. Her daughter's future was assured—and it was its own kind of justice, of compensation for all that had been taken from them. She knew her daughter would bring light to all the dark corners of MacAdder Castle. Just as long as Rhona herself never had to set foot there again.

The guard went on. "Let the one seeking justice step forward and take her due."

Broden whispered, "Stand tall, sister. Ye deserve this."

Rhona looked from her brother to her husband. "I don't understand. Women don't get due justice."

"That needs to change," Royce said. "My wife gets due justice."

"I wrote to King Alexander demanding restitution for all that happened once I learned the truth of the first forged betrothal agreement," Broden explained. "The king's guard arrived last night, and we hunted MacAdders today. Ironic that we found them after they left here."

Rhona stood tall, looking at Malcolm and Simon, suddenly understanding her brother's and her husband's bruised knuckles. The battered faces of the two on trial looked more afraid than she ever would have guessed. Completely different from the smug faces they'd worn earlier.

Malcolm wasn't smirking now.

That alone was worth coming outside to see.

Broden took Rhona's hand and marched her to stand in front of the two men. "The MacAdders are charged with fabricating a document twelve years ago, forcing my sister Rhona to marry Duncan MacAdder. Who wrote the document?"

Malcolm said, "Duncan did. It was all his idea."

Broden dropped his sister's hand so he and Royce could take two steps closer to the men, something they did in unison. "I'll ask ye for the truth again. Who wrote this document?"

Simon's face paled when he looked at Broden and at his fists. Then he said, "I did."

Royce asked, "And who forged Donnel Shaw's signature on that document?"

Malcolm said, "I did."

Rhona squared her shoulders and managed to control the tears that begged to be set free.

Ainsley's voice came from behind her. "Who forged King Alexander's signature on the document that was brought to my sister today claiming the king was to annul her marriage to Royce MacRob and force her to marry Malcolm MacAdder?"

Neither answered.

"Did Duncan do that, too, from beyond the grave?" Broden jeered.

Royce's fury brought him to the two men, his voice ringing out louder than any others. "Who dared to tell my wife that they were going to annul our marriage?"

Malcolm meekly answered, "I did, but Simon helped!"

"Shut your mouth!" Simon snarled. "'Twas all your doing!"

The king's captain said, "We will find the truth of it when we have them in the dungeon in Edinburgh. Forging the king's signature on an unauthorized order is considered treason."

The crowd cheered. Rhona nodded in satisfaction. "Good. Let the guards take them, get them off our land."

"Do ye no' want to take yer just due?" Royce asked. "Ye were ready to boil them in oil no' so long ago."

"I don't understand. What does that mean?"

"Rhona, ye may do as ye wish to both men," Broden said. Her brother looked like he was trying to suppress an evil grin. "Ye have the right to stab them anywhere but their belly or their face. Ye can hit them, kick them, do whatever ye wish to do as long as ye dinnae kill them."

She looked at her brother. "I cannot do such a thing."

Broden took her hand and said, "Ye must do something. They deserve all of it, but it will ease some of yer pain if ye get the chance for just due. I believe restitution can help ye heal."

She looked to Royce. "I cannot punch either of them. That would mean touching them. They're too disgusting to get so close to."

Royce said, "Ye told me how much ye hated them, how much ye hated Duncan. I wish ye to close yer eyes and go back to the night Duncan had them hold ye down so he could beat ye. Recall what they did."

She closed her eyes and thought of all that had happened.

Ainsley leaned forward and said, "May I do it for her?"

Broden's eyes widened, but he nodded. "If Rhona agrees, then aye."

Ainsley said, "Ye just finished telling me how they stomped on yer breast and punched ye in yer female parts, did ye no'?"

Rhona nodded, and all her fury came back to her. "Aye, I did. You get Simon, Ainsley. Malcolm will be mine."

Royce leaned forward and hugged her quickly. "Good. I like that. I'm proud of ye, lass."

Ainsley strode over to Simon, took a firm hold of one of his nipples, then squeezed hard and twisted. He released a cry of pain. Then, without letting go, she punched him in the face. The force of the blow jerked his body, and he screamed, then settled into a whimper. Ainsley whispered something in his ear, then stepped back.

Rhona strode over to Malcolm and stood in front of him, remembering exactly what he'd done. But then she turned around and looked at Royce.

"I cannot do it." She'd never been a physically violent person and didn't know how to become one. Malcolm MacAdder wasn't worth changing her nature. She took one more look at the devil and shook her head, turning away.

The man disgusted her. She had no desire to touch him.

Malcolm said, "I knew you couldn't. You are too weak. I told Duncan he should have beat you more."

Rhona saw red. She turned slowly and stared at Malcolm. How cruel he'd been to her when she'd been married, how much he'd frightened her earlier in the day.

"Let's see how strong you are, then." She spat in his face, then bent at her waist and kicked her leg out with all her strength, hitting him directly in the bollocks. She stepped back for a moment and then kicked him with her other foot, delivering a double blow. Malcolm screamed, convulsed in agony, vomited, then passed out.

Justice was served.

She spun on the heel of her boot and walked back to her husband. She was surprised to see that he looked a little pale. "I love you, Royce MacRob."

"No one will ever take ye away from me, Rhona. And after seeing that, no one will ever try."

The king's men took the pair away.

"Just a moment," she whispered to Royce.

She strode over to her brother and said, "Many thanks for whatever part you had in getting me my just due. You're a fine laird, Broden. Da would be proud of you."

"I had to do something after all they put ye through. I had no idea what ye were subjected to. To hear the truth of the matter was more than I could handle. Had I known, I would have torn down the castle walls and taken ye away myself. Now it is done, and I wish ye much happiness with Royce. Ye are where ye belong."

"And you know you and Catlin are welcome anytime. In fact, I see her coming now with Giric. Please stay for the evening meal. I wish to get to know my clan again, but more than anyone, my brother and his new wife, and Ainsley's new husband. Could we all spend more time together?"

"I think we would all like that." Broden kissed

Catlin, who had just stepped into his encircling arm.

Tor was teasing Ainsley about punching Simon, kissing her knuckles. Forsy, Helen, and Annie came across the courtyard, and Rhona blessed her lucky stars that Annie had not been witness to all that had just happened.

Royce bent down and allowed Annie to climb onto his shoulders. She giggled uncontrollably. Rhona vowed to raise her child in such a way that she kept her bright disposition, her unstinting love and sense of fun. It would serve her well in fifteen years' time.

"Truly, Broden. That is the sound I wish to hear more of—laughter."

EPILOGUE

Ten years later

"RHONA, ARE YE ready yet? The lads are anxious to go." Royce paced in the great hall, yelling to his wife. He glanced over at their two sons, who were feinting at each other with their practice swords.

Rhys had been born nine months after they married.

Four months after she gave birth to Rhys, she'd come down to Royce one morn and had a bowl of porridge, only to heave it back into her bowl. She'd managed a smile and said quietly, "Congratulations, Royce. We're due to have our second bairn in about eight moons."

He'd been so excited that he'd picked her up and tossed her in the air, and she'd promptly vomited all over the floor, barely missing him.

He couldn't help but laugh over that memory. Life with Rhona had been as wonderful as he'd known it would be. Oh, they'd had their moments when their two stubborn personalities had clashed, but that was what made their relationship so special.

They'd lived without each other for long enough to appreciate what they had. He would be forever grateful, of that much he was certain.

Annie came down the stairs and said, "She's nearly done."

Rhys hurried over, his blue eyes showing his wish to hurry, his mahogany-colored hair tied back at his nape. Their eldest son was the image of Rhona, and Lachlan looked just like the MacRobs. "She's coming at last? I've been ready to go for the longest time. Lachlan and I will beat all the Shaws this year."

He and his brother spent hours training with Mungo and Struan, perfecting their swordplay, archery, and riding.

As usual, Annie gave it back to the boys. "Mayhap I dinnae wish for ye to beat the Shaws. Mayhap I'll be on a Shaw team this year." Then she smirked and looked at Royce just before standing on her tiptoes to plant a kiss on her adopted father's cheek. She whispered in his ear, "I would never do that, Da."

"I would understand. 'Tis fine with me if ye choose to play both sides. Both sides are in yer heart."

Annie, quick as ever, replied, "And they are both in yer heart. Ye just choose no' to admit it."

"Right ye are. But 'tis almost time for ye to take up yer MacAdder side, as well. That castle is rightfully yers, lassie."

"No' yet, Da."

Rhona came down the stairs, beautiful as ever. He couldn't take his eyes off her swaying hips, her soft curves, but it was always the love in her eyes that entranced him.

"Mama, are ye ready? We must practice on the obstacle course first," Lachlan said.

"Ye'll have plenty of time to practice." She kissed his forehead and he wiped it away, rolling his eyes.

They headed out of the great hall, not surprised to find Tor and Ainsley waiting, their six bairns running in circles around the two in the middle of the courtyard.

"Another kitten?" Royce nodded to Tor and Ainsley's eldest. The girl had seen eight summers and reminded him of his brother in many ways.

"If ye will believe it," Tor said, "she found the wee one on the road here. I told her 'twould no' be possible to travel with a kitten but . . ."

Tor exchanged a glance with his wife. One that still warmed Royce's heart to see. The love between him and Ainsley had given him four nieces and two nephews.

"Ye look at me," Ainsley said to her husband, "as if I bid her keep it. If ye tell our daughter nay when she asks for aught these next few days, I'll carry the wee kitten home myself."

His brother did not even attempt to hold back his laughter. "Ye've the right of it," he admitted. "No' my daughter nor my wife."

Hell, no one wanted to see this, but his brother's affection for his wife was well known. Even now, as he kissed her thoroughly for all to witness, none paid them mind, accustomed to such a display.

"Mother." Tor and Ainsley's eldest son tugged

on his mother's gown. "Who do ye wish will win this day?"

Tor grabbed his son and hoisted him into the air, the boy squealing in delight as his father brought him back down to the ground. "The MacRobs, of course," he said, eliciting cries of revolt among his children. All began to talk at once as they resumed their play.

"I will cheer for my children, and my nephews," Ainsley said to her son. Seemingly satisfied, he scampered away.

"I stand tall and proud when I'm newly born, yet I get shorter as I grow old. What am I?"

Niall, Broden and Catlin's eldest lad, crossed his arms and waited, a proud look on his face for the riddle he'd just composed.

Of course, Broden didn't miss the light of recognition that almost instantly lit Laila's bright green eyes. At seven summers, she was two years younger than Niall, but she'd most assuredly been gifted her mother's sharp wits, and could rival her older brother when they sparred with riddles.

Catlin must have noted Laila's immediate comprehension as well, for as the lass opened her mouth to shout the answer, she cut in: "Let yer wee brothers have a chance to ponder it as well, sweet."

But while Broden and Catlin and their two elder bairns sat on the raised dais in Castle Shaw's great hall, their younger two, Aiden and Rabbie, were wrestling amongst the rushes on the floor. Broden couldn't help but snort. Aye, they took more after him, and from their fighting spirit, both would be fine warriors someday. If they didn't strangle each other first.

Unable to contain the answer any longer, Laila blurted, "A candle! Ye are a candle!"

Niall grinned. "Aye, ye got me."

"Come, my wee army of Shaws," Broden said, standing. "We'll be late for the festivities, which willnae do as we are the hosts this year. What is more, ye lot represent the clan, and I willnae have bairns of mine losing to a bunch of MacRobs."

Catlin swatted his arm, but then gladly accepted his offered hand. As he levered her to her feet, she muttered an oath about this being the last time.

She was round as the moon with their fifth bairn, and swore every time she was forced to stand that she would never again share a bed with Broden. Then again, she'd said the same after Aiden, and Rabbie, but the bond between her and Broden was far too strong to be held at bay for long.

Broden could only smile at his sharp-tongued wife. He gave her a reassuring kiss on her forehead, then looped her arm through his as he guided her down from the dais.

"I'll be sure to find ye a comfortable chair to watch the obstacle course, love."

She glanced at him out of the corner of her eye. "And a footstool?"

"Aye, and a footstool. Aught ye wish, my bonnie wife."

Now she blessed him with a true smile, and he felt as if the sun were shining on him, as it always did whenever she was near.

"Will Quinn and Sorley be there, Da?" Niall asked as he fell in behind them.

"And Ella and Glynnis?" Laila added.

"Aye, all of Ian and Marta's bairns will be there," Broden replied. "They are coming all the way to the castle for the festivities."

"Good, because we'll need them on the Shaw side if we are to best the MacRobs."

"Dinnae forget ye are half MacRob, Niall," Catlin said dryly over her shoulder. "Aiden, Rabbie! Come along."

As the younger lads tumbled out of the great hall after them, Niall carried on. "Aye, but I am to be the Shaw laird someday, isnae that right? And ye always told me my name means 'champion.' So it is only right that I lead the Shaws to victory today. Isnae that what ye told me, Da?"

That earned him another swat from Catlin, but Broden could only chuckle. "Well, he's no' wrong," he offered to his frowning wife.

"We are family," Catlin said, glancing at each one of her children in turn. "With the MacRobs as well as the Shaws. Let us all remember that in the excitement of the festival."

"Aye, Mama," they replied in unison.

"Good," Catlin said, her emerald eyes taking on a sly twinkle. "Now let's go show my beloved MacRob family what strong stuff we Shaws are made of."

~

It was near the end of the festival, the last game on the last day. One lad in green plaid shoved a lad in a blue plaid, who was immediately joined by a lass in a gown of blue plaid, and that was when Royce smiled, crossing his arms and leaning back with pride. He knew if his sire were here, he'd be as proud as Royce was to see his Rhys stand tall against another trying to change the results.

One shove brought another, and before they knew it, the argument had become a brawl of lads and lasses swinging and shouting at each other.

"We won!"

"Nay, ye didnae. The Shaws won!"

"Nay, the MacRobs are always the best. Shaws are losers."

Royce wrapped his arm around his wife's shoulder, then glanced over at Broden. "Some things never change, do they, Shaw?"

Broden shook his head, grinned, and said, "MacRob, I couldnae be more proud."

THE END

www.keiramontclair.com

If you enjoyed this trilogy, then try our Enchanted Falls Trilogy available at Amazon.

NOVELS BY KEIRA MONTCLAIR

HIGHLAND HEALERS
THE CURSE OF BLACK ISLE
THE WITCH OF BLACK ISLE
THE SCOURGE OF BLACK ISLE
THE GHOSTS OF BLACK ISLE

THE CLAN GRANT SERIES
#1- RESCUED BY A HIGHLANDER-
Alex and Maddie
#2- HEALING A HIGHLANDER'S HEART-
Brenna and Quade
#3- LOVE LETTERS FROM LARGS-
Brodie and Celestina
#4-JOURNEY TO THE HIGHLANDS-
Robbie and Caralyn
#5-HIGHLAND SPARKS-
Logan and Gwyneth
#6-MY DESPERATE HIGHLANDER-
Micheil and Diana
#7-THE BRIGHTEST STAR IN THE
HIGHLANDS-
Jennie and Aedan
#8- HIGHLAND HARMONY-
Avelina and Drew
#9-YULETIDE ANGELS

ABOUT THE AUTHOR

KEIRA MONTCLAIR IS the pen name of an author who lives in South Carolina with her husband. She loves to write fast-paced, emotional romance, especially with children as secondary characters.

When she's not writing, she loves to spend time with her grandchildren. She's worked as a high school math teacher, a registered nurse, and an office manager. She loves ballet, mathematics, puzzles, learning anything new, and creating new characters for her readers to fall in love with.

She writes historical romantic suspense. Her best-selling series is a family saga that follows two medieval Scottish clans through four generations and now numbers over thirty books.

~

Contact her through her website:
keiramontclair.com.

Made in the USA
Monee, IL
16 October 2022

16014175R00142